GussyFlo Publishing

ISBN: 978-1-956798-01-2

*For Gustavia*

# YOU COULD DO
# *damage*

### RENÉE A. MOSES

# ONE

## Gianna

"Look who finally made it. The guest of honor." Trish stood and hugged me tightly.

"Heyyy!" The constant smiling hurt my cheeks.

Sienna, who'd recently gotten promoted to my boss, was trying to murder a Mariah Carey song on the small stage area, but it was killing her. Being a non-singer from birth, Carey might have been the worst choice. However, my girl stuck with it even when her voice cracked at pretty much every high note.

Trish shoved me a step backward. "Uh, all of this is for you. How you this late?"

My hands flew up in surrender before the shots flew my way. "Something came up at the last minute. I did my best not to get here too late. I'm so sorry."

We ducked when Sienna missed another note. It sounded like a cry for help. The girl rubbed her neck and continued. We laughed so hard I thought it'd broken the stank mood for a second.

"Mmhm." Trish threw me some side-eye. "That beautiful sound is what you've been missing."

"Shit, I think I should've waited longer. Matter fact, I'm gonna walk out and come back in like two minutes when the song is over."

"Ha! You wrong for that. She's the one who put this together. So, we gotta take it."

"Do we though?" I turned to walk away until Trish hit my elbow. I faced her. "I'm playing. As long as I missed your set, the worst is over."

"I hate you."

"I love you." I blew her a kiss.

Trish cussed me out with one finger and sipped her drink. That big, bowl-looking glass full of some green concoction grabbed my attention. "Oooh, what's that?"

"You'd know if yo' ass was here on time." Lonnie snuck up on me. I hadn't even felt her presence.

"Not you too. I said I'm sorry. I texted your butt the whole time."

"It still doesn't excuse it." She bumped my shoulder before hugging me. "But you're here now. The food should be out in a minute. We were going to starve to death waiting on you." My eyes hurt with all the rolling of them that they had me doing.

Sienna finished the homicide to our ears and joined in on the tardy roasting after greeting me. Then she had the nerve to brag about singing better than any of us. Girlie must've burst her own eardrums and couldn't hear worth a damn anymore. I didn't even have to come at her because Lonnie's impression of Sienna that sounded like a cat running around on fire was spot on.

While laughing 'til it hurt, a platter of food magically fell onto my lap. Well, a server placed it on the table in front of me. I'd built up one hell of an appetite on my way here.

"He must've put it on your ass to be this late and this

hungry." Lonnie called me out after my third hot wing in less than a minute.

My trainer turned...whatever. We didn't have titles. We weren't together. We simply did things together, usually with no clothes.

His last-minute text an hour before I would've left to come here caught me off guard. He'd offered to give me a proper send-off. And that he did.

I told the girls I'd be ten minutes late. That ten turned into forty-five. We had this room for two hours. Unfortunately for them, I used a good chunk of it on one thing I'd miss the most.

"Look, I will make it up to y'all. I promise."

Trish twisted her neck too fast for it not to have hurt. "How? You have a morning flight."

"I ain't flying the plane. All I gotta do is be there on time. Sober or not."

Trish squealed. "Awww shit! Let's hit up a strip club like we used to do before Miss Designated Driver got married. And if her ass can't go, we're dropping her off."

Lonnie laughed and gave her a high five. They needed to leave Sienna alone. She'd found her in-home striptease. We'd make the best of the time we had singing. Then off to see some nakedness!

The last hour passed by so fast. I stayed true to my limits and stuck with Monica songs. I hit most of her notes. After butchering everything from Mary J. Blige to Bone-Thugs-n-Harmony—we had to do "Crossroads" one time— we said our goodbye to the newlywed, and headed to the best end of my last night in Miami.

My sperm donor, Blair, picked me up from the airport. We stopped by my new condo, thanks to him. When your father was an orthopedic surgeon full of guilt, you got condos and other grandiose shit you didn't ask for. It was his way of saying he was sorry.

The place was spectacular; and I'd accepted it, but insisted on paying for everything else. Hell, I still drove the Audi he'd bought as a graduation gift. Blair needed to understand that I was an adult with a career I was in love with. I could take care of myself.

I promised to have dinner with him on my first night. So, we did a quick walk-through of my condo before we hopped back into the car to head to his house.

The rest of my blood relatives lived in a mini-mansion with Blair. I reminded him of the castle-like feature in front of the house. He hated it, but his new wife had to have it. And since it didn't come with an out-of-reach price tag, he caved in order to make her happy.

Blair took it seriously to live beneath his means in many areas. He enjoyed the simple things. From what he'd told me, his first house was over the top. This time around, he went a different route.

After the divorce from his first wife, he despised anything too lavish. That woman spoiled him on the idea of splurging. Even after she remarried and he no longer had to pay alimony, he kept that extra money in the bank.

The only time he spent big was on any occasion to bestow gifts on those he loved and on vacations. Since he'd established a relationship with me, I'd been on at least one family vacation each year. Those never got old.

We'd gone to London, Ghana, Fiji, Paris, and a few others. I only wished my mom was there, so I wouldn't feel like such an outsider. Then again, my bestie, Janelle, started tagging along two years ago.

Shana, Blair's latest wife, embraced me inside the house like she hadn't seen me in years. She was cool as hell. Maybe because she was twelve years younger than Blair. Only in her forties, the woman looked like my damn sister. She was fortunate enough to be gorgeous on the inside and out. Unlike that witch he'd married when I was a kid.

My little half-siblings ran to meet me at the door and almost knocked me down.

"Gia! Gia! We missed you," they echoed in the foyer.

"I missed you guys, too," I sang before the hugs, kisses, and tickles.

Olivia, who was almost seven, pulled me upstairs to see the massive dollhouse in her room. She'd talked about it so much, so I'd promised I'd play with her as soon as I got back to Houston.

Twenty minutes in, Shana announced that dinner was ready. We were a little bummed. Olivia was so fun and silly. She thought I was the most entertaining person on the planet. She always brought out the kid in me.

Everyone got cleaned up and sat at the smaller dining table near the kitchen. The massive table in the dining room was for formal occasions.

Shana prepared her famous seafood lasagna. Well, famous in the family. The woman had the skills of a world-renowned chef. She would've been until Blair swept her off her feet

"Are you excited? You're back home for good!" Shana smiled so hard it was contagious.

"I am for the most part. It is a bit weird, you know. Being here when the people I left aren't anymore." I had to take a breath. "Yeah, I'm still excited."

She and Blair shared a look. He covered my hand with his. "Your mother and grandmother would be so proud of you, Gia. No, they *are* proud of you."

"Yeah." I cleared my throat. "So, Jonah! What have you been up to? Your dad told me you are into coding now."

My little brother helped shift the energy of the room. He talked all about this new game that also taught coding and how much he loved it. He'd been to a camp earlier this summer and was really into it.

"Oooh! I got a big shrimp!" Olivia announced before dropping it into her mouth.

"Girl, you should've bit that one." I watched as she struggled to close her mouth with the first few chews. We didn't need any choking going on.

"You're ready for the new company?" Blair gulped his wine and held the glass.

"I think so. Everybody seemed nice during the interviews. Let's hope that's the normal vibe there."

"I pray so. Some people are so ugly when they don't have to be. I pray you'll have to deal with little or none of them. One woman I used to work with came in mad at the world every morning. Imagine the energy it takes to maintain such a funky attitude all day, every day," Blair said.

"Ugh! I hate those types. But I won't let them rub that energy off on me if they are there. I'm ready for a new chapter."

Shana grinned. "Does this new chapter include a new boyfriend?"

"Ewww," the kids whined.

"That *is* nasty." I winked at them. "I don't want to go down that road yet. Or ever. I simply want to have fun and be free."

Blair lowered his head. "I don't even want to know what that means."

Shana and I met eyes and giggled. "No, you don't, old man."

"I most certainly am not. See?" He flexed his biceps.

"Being fit doesn't knock that number down. No matter how many muscles you got, you still old," I reminded him. The kids laughed with their "oohs" since they wouldn't say that to him.

"I mean, you do have a twenty-eight-year-old daughter, sweetheart. You might not want to fight that battle."

"Aww, naw! You got my lady against me, too? You don't call me old when I—"

Shana gasped so loud. "Blair!"

"Okay, now see that right there definitely deserves an ew."

Blair sat back in his chair. "What? I was going to say work for so many hours. Y'all the nasty ones. Mind all in the gutter."

"Oh, please." Shana stood up to clear the table. I helped her. Then she pulled out a cheesecake from the fridge. She pointed to the platter of toppings next to it for me to get. We set it all on the table.

Shana threw down with any cuisine. Dinner with the family would be one perk of being back home that I would enjoy the hell out of.

After dessert, we spent the rest of the night playing in the ridiculous game room. First foosball, then pool, a few arcade games, and finally our favorite pastime: puzzles. Something about them kept our interest long enough to sit and just be together.

Against my initial wishes and after some begging from

Jonah and Olivia, I stayed the night. We got ready for bed and slept on the floor in the theater.

It wasn't the worst idea since my furniture wouldn't arrive until tomorrow afternoon. After that, I'd bother Janelle, who I'd forgotten to call back after I landed.

## TWO

# Gianna

"Don't even start with me. We were supposed to meet up yesterday, but you stood me up." Janelle backed away from my hug.

"What did you want me to do? When I had time, you were busy with your boo. I tried."

"Heifer, please. You been back for two days and this is my first time seeing you."

"Uh, you could've come to me too."

"Yeah, yeah. Well, you're here now. So, give me your funky ol' hug."

This time I backed away. "Forget you." I pushed her forehead before she hit my arm.

Janelle was my sister from another mister. All the way. Since the sixth grade, we'd been besties. Her mother and mine grew close over time because of us. So, we did almost everything together growing up.

"You want to sit at the bar?" She hooked my arm as we walked into Cringo's Mexican Kitchen.

"Nope! I'm too hungry and I don't want nobody watching me stuff my face."

"But I have to, soooo?" Janelle shrugged.

"Oh, shut up."

We followed the hostess to our table. It was a late lunch date since my new job didn't start until next week, and Janelle's work hours were all over the place sometimes.

"Girl! I cannot believe you're here." She quickly tapped her feet repeatedly on the floor.

"Me neither. It's been so long."

A waitress introduced herself before taking our order.

"So, what's next? You unpacked yet?"

I chuckled. "Only some of my clothes."

"What! You need help?"

"Maybe. I'm not in the mood right now. I've been sleeping and reading."

She rolled her eyes. "Of course, you have. That's all you do. You need to get a life outside those books."

How dare she? "Excuse me. I have a life. A good one. And I also enjoy a book when my amazing life gives me the time."

"Mmhmm, sure."

"I can't with you. Your ass need to pick up a book now and then."

"I do! I'm trying to learn how to cook. My mom don't make everything I like. I've been meaning to take Shana up on her offer to teach me a little something, but that was kind of weird with you not being here at first."

"Nah, it's weird because you still crushing on her husband."

She burst out laughing and so did I. "I mean, your dad is fine as hell. But I got a man."

"Obviously. That's why you blew me off yesterday. You were probably busy getting off with Mr. Cameron."

"Eww! Well..." She tilted her head to the side with a

brief smirk.

"Ha! See."

"Anyway, we can do something this weekend. And in the meantime, you need to unpack, so I can see your place. I bet it's nice with a rich ass daddy picking it out."

"Girl! He be doing too much. However, I ain't mad at the place. Two bedrooms, two baths, a gourmet kitchen. I mean, 'cause a girl like me can cook."

"I'm the one with a man." She poked her lips at me.

"Uh, you're the only one who wants one. I don't need that kind of distraction in my life. I'm gonna get my money up, travel the world on my dime, and be free to do whomever and whatever I want."

"Right until those eggs crack, then you'll change your mind."

"Whatever, I don't—"

"Ooooh!" we said in unison as the woman delivered our humongous margaritas.

We sipped until we were content.

Janelle got off of my back and talked about Cameron. He seemed like a nice guy, and I was genuinely happy for her because she wanted love and all that.

Love left my mom pregnant and alone when Blair didn't return her feelings. Then the struggle began for her. I promised her and myself I wouldn't walk the same path. My grandmother had raised my mother alone, too. I wanted no parts of love.

---

"Damn, girl. That was...shit!" D'Mario fell back onto the pillow next to me, damn near panting.

D'Mario had booked the room after a quick conversation. By the vibes of his profile, he was easy picking. The details got the least of my attention. His name and age were second to the dark chocolate complexion chiseled in a way that was best for eye candy. That was all I needed to see. One swipe later, he tried to tell me about his current situation. I only wanted one thing from him. Talking wasn't it.

Two hours later, we met at the Omni Hotel near the Galleria. When I got to the room, this man put his picture to shame. Sometimes these dudes be false advertising with old photos. The last time that happened to me, I booked it before the guy opened the door fully.

I caught my breath and sat up to put my clothes back on. After grabbing my things, I disappeared to the bathroom. Minutes later, I re-entered the bedroom, dressed to go.

"Where are you going?" D'Mario willed himself up and leaned against the headboard.

"Home."

"You don't want to stay and have breakfast or something in the morning?"

Putting on my watch and picking up my purse, I gave him a dry smile. "I'm not spending the night."

"So, you really gon' use me for sex and bounce?"

I giggled at him sounding like he was hurt. "There was no gun to your head. We both benefited from where I stand."

Before I reached the door, D'Mario hopped out of bed butt-ass naked. "Wait! What if I wanted another round?"

My eyes met the only thing that I'd stay for. The size had me salivating even while resting, but this bout had exhausted him. And sleeping in his arms was never part of the deal, even for half an hour.

He must've seen me staring at it. The smirk on his face

showed his pride in his piece. Well-deserved pride. "I can be ready after a quick nap. That nut took a lot out of me. Give me a minute and—"

"I had a great time and I am not against doing it again some other time. I need to get going."

"You got a man, don't you?"

I burst out laughing. "That's none of your business."

"Okay, but stay with me."

"You don't even know me. What if I'm crazy?"

"Hell, I wouldn't put it past you. Any woman that can tire my ass out like that might have a crazy side. I can handle it. Trust me."

"I'm good. Sooo, I will text you later." I opened the door and stepped into the hall. No way he'd plead with me out there. I winked and closed the door behind me.

On the ride home, I stopped by Jack in the Box for some tacos and jalapeno poppers. D'Mario did what I needed him to do. Now, I required food. It wasn't even midnight on this late Friday, so I called my boo Janelle. Luckily, her hot date with the allblk channel was still in full swing.

My place looked like a tornado of boxes had hit it. The boxes were still in the same place the movers had dropped them in last week.

Settling in at work with so many faces to remember, having dinner with Blair almost every other night, plus being horny as shit on the others, no time seemed like the right time to unpack. After nearly doing an accidental back-flip on a small box I didn't see yesterday, I needed to get on that before I became a casualty to my clutter.

Janelle answered the door wrapped in a blanket with bugged-out eyes at the sight of my bag. "Don't get excited. This is for me, chica."

Her head jerked back with no words. Then that heifer

snatched my bag and ran to the couch. "You play too damn much."

"Ninja please! You can't come in here with Jack in the Crack and not share. Whatchu think this is?"

"If I knew yo' greedy ass wanted some, I would've gotten extra." After locking the door, I ran up on her and got my bag back. She'd already stolen a taco.

I sat and removed the contents of my bag, setting them on the coffee table. "What we watching?"

"A pig eating."

"What the hell is that?"

Janelle switched her whole body in my direction and pointed the remote at me. "About a selfish so-called friend who didn't bring me no food."

"Damn, if it's that serious, you can have some." I opened the jalapeno poppers container.

She lifted the little box, looking under it. "Where's the buttermilk ranch?"

That question made me snatch at my bag to search even though I'd emptied it seconds ago. "Dammit, man."

"You didn't check before you left?"

"Does it look like I checked, roach?"

"You the damn roach. With yo' stingy ass."

I lifted my hands halfway in the air. "It's only ranch. Why you in your feelings?"

"Only ranch?! Only ranch?!" Janelle said, like Jim Mora's famous "Playoffs?!" rant. I burst out laughing and so did she.

"Yeah, you right. We need to go back. I can't eat these with no regular ranch."

This girl didn't even change. She threw on her slippers and we walked to my car while I hid my face with embarrassment. Janelle still wore that damn blanket. Her place was cold enough for it, but the humidity outside was thick as usual. She looked crazy.

We got more food and demanded extra buttermilk ranch for the treachery of leaving it out the first time. When we returned, the TV was blasting in her apartment.

"Didn't you turn it off?" I asked since I might've been wrong. It for damn sure wasn't that loud.

"I thought so." Janelle unlocked the door, and we entered, finding allblk was off, but Joe Budden's podcast had somehow gotten on.

She located the remote that had mysteriously moved and turned it down. "You got a roommate you didn't tell me about?"

"Yeah, right." She walked to the bedroom and came back. "Ain't nobody in here. The door was locked. Zak probably came, saw I wasn't here and left. I hate when he does that."

I shrugged it off, still hungry as hell. Janelle went to the kitchen to get us some juice, and I repeated the same steps of removing the food from the bag earlier. I had plenty of ranch for my poppers this time. I sat down and slid the container we left on the table my way, but it moved too quickly. "Aw, hell naw! Who the hell ate my food?"

"Stop playing." She came into the living room with two full cups.

"Does it look like I'm playing?"

"How the  "

"Ahhh!" Somebody yelled like a maniac and jumped out of the hallway.

Both of us screamed with juice splattering on the floor and table. My body turned automatically to face the culprit in a stance that looked like I could fight. By the size of this man, I'd lose.

# THREE

## Gianna

"WHAT THE FUCK IS WRONG WITH YOU? I HATE YOU," Janelle yelled, holding her chest with one hand and the other rested on her forehead.

"Who the hell is this?" I yelled, still on alert. My whole body itched in places I could never scratch when I got scared.

The guy stepped closer to me. I moved. "Back the hell up off me. I don't know you."

"So, you move to Florida for a few years and now you don't know nobody."

I squinted my eyes at him for a better look. When he smiled, I rolled my eyes. He had the same smirk as a familiar little asshole used to. Well, big asshole, this time around. He towered over me when he got close enough.

"Zakari." My tepid tone gave off my irritation.

Zak sucked his teeth. "You ain't gotta sound so excited." He hugged me too tight and even picked me up.

"Put me down, dumbass."

He chuckled after dropping me on the couch. "Same old attitude."

I scoffed. "Same old idiot." His gaze held mine a little too long when I finally made it back onto my feet.

I couldn't stand Zakari. He embodied a pest to the highest power. Being the only child, I never realized that little brothers could be such little assholes. The pranks, attitudes, and annoying antics surpassed what I'd assumed from TV. Zak was a pain.

By the eighth grade, Zak became more of a nuisance to me than to Janelle. She only laughed because she had the new privilege of not being his target. Their mother, Ms. Jenae, got on him when she was present, but parents were usually blind to it.

By senior year, Zak had grown into a monster since we all attended Willowridge High School. He was only two grades behind us. I'd gotten used to him being annoying, but in high school we had foul mouths with no adults in earshot. We ranked on each other so much that everyone knew we hated each other.

I remember when Janelle's family came to my house for pictures before we left for prom night, dateless. That little bastard called me the frog prince, saying no one asked me out because I looked like a man. I laughed my ass off at first, then it bothered me the whole night. I was very athletic, but my body looked nothing like a dude's. I still wondered like an idiot.

"What are you doing here, Zak?" Janelle inquired.

"No, screw that! Did you eat my poppers?" I held the empty box near his face.

"Oh, those were yours?"

I sucked my teeth. "You are still the same. No respect. You need to go get me some more."

"I ain't doing that."

My jaw fell open. I wanted to punch him. As I looked

for the perfect spot to hit, I got distracted. The shirt he wore initially appeared loose, but it hugged his biceps. Where did he get those from? His hair was a mess at the top, but faded everywhere else. No more braces to clown him for.

The man standing before me was far from the little boy I'd happily left behind eight years ago. I came to Houston two years ago, but I was too preoccupied to notice him. Zak had me looking tonight.

The air thickened and the temp inched hotter. I blamed the tats almost covering both of his forearms or his perfect fitting jeans that weren't those silly ass skinny ones or too big, hanging off his ass. The chain hanging around his neck did something to me because it stopped right above his defined pecs.

Oooh, his lips. They were barely pink, mostly caramel like the rest of his skin. Did he put baby oil on or something? It looked like his skin glistened. Facial hair too. And it didn't have patches. He had a perfect beard, neatly trimmed down. Who the hell was this man?

"Gia?...Gia? Helloooo?" Janelle waved her hand in my face.

I twitched. "Huh? What happened?"

"What happened to *you*?" Janelle asked.

Zakari laughed. "I think she's checking out the goods. You can touch them if you want."

I narrowed my eyes at him. "Ain't nobody thinking about you."

"Ha! I see you looking. Stop lying to yourself." He licked his stupid, bite-worthy lips.

"Fine, I was. Only to plot your disappearance for eating my damn food. I really wanted those."

"Is it really that serious?" Zak asked.

"Yes!" Janelle and I yelled.

"Damn, I'll go get some. Ain't it too late for you to be eating this junk, anyway?"

"Boy, get yo' ass on and get her food."

"Y'all trippin' for real. All the food in these bags and you want more?"

We said nothing. We only folded our arms and stared Zakari down until he threw his hands up and claimed he'd be right back. We cleaned up the mess before Janelle changed her clothes.

I had to warm up my taco from my first trip. Janelle bit into her sourdough burger and froze in what appeared to be an erotic pleasure. She caught me staring.

"What? It's been so long since I had one of these. I try to eat right. This food is all the way wrong."

"No, you having an orgasm over a sloppy burger is wrong."

"Whatever. Mind yo' business."

I sat in the recliner, trying to muffle my smile by stuffing my face. "I haven't seen your brother in forever. That little bastard grew up on me. Trying to look like a grown man."

She rolled her eyes. "He don't act like one. He does that a lot."

"What?"

"Scare the shit out of me. I gave him a key to my apartment for emergencies only. Apparently, he thinks jumping out of dark corners and hallways is important."

I couldn't help but laugh at the image. From how that fool popped out on us, catching someone alone was worse.

"That ain't funny. He's lucky I don't have a weapon in here."

I finished my taco and moved on to bacon cheddar potato wedges. After I smothered them in the ranch, it was on. I had to be careful not to sound too satisfied like she did minutes ago. "Why won't you get the key back?"

"I tried. He won't give it."

"What you mean he won't give it? Take it back."

"You saw his big ass. I can't bully him like I used to."

"'Cause you's a punk."

She laughed out loud. "Then you get it since you so tough."

"I will."

Janelle's phone rang. Less than a minute into her call, she told me Zak had my food outside. He was running late for something and didn't want to waste time bringing the food in.

When I walked out the door, I followed the vibration of banging music. The kind that made you swear the loudness would break the car down. This negro held my food out the window. I stood still to show that he was not about to rush me.

"Come on, girl."

"You come on. You're the one who ate my food."

"Damn, the stubbornness didn't wear off by now."

"Neither did your assholeness."

"Oh, we making up words now?"

"Same as you pretending to be late to anything in the middle of the night. You just lazy."

"I ain't lying about shit. Duty calls."

"Duty?"

"Hell, yeah. A girl I've been tryna smash is throwing it at me right now. I gotta go catch it. And you are keeping her waiting."

Zak tossed the bag toward me. I caught it before it hit the ground.

"Nice catch, prince." He winked and drove off.

"You little motherfucker."

---

MY PLACE LOOKED GOOD. IT ACTUALLY FELT LIKE home. My office resembled a functioning one. The two bookshelves did their job holding all of my books and binders. Sheer curtains hung over the window. Blair found some type of hanging rods that required no nails. They worked great and put a smile on his face for another thing he'd taught me.

He and Janelle started early with me to get my place in order. Janelle only came because Blair promised to take us out to brunch afterward.

"You think you have enough books?" Janelle asked after opening another box full of them.

That was my mother's doing. She always had a book in her hand and I adopted that habit. I had her collection and the many books I've picked up over the years. I cringed every time I heard of another bookstore closing. Nothing could beat walking into a chain or mom-and-pop bookstore and touching the merchandise before buying. Sometimes I knew exactly what I needed, and other times—the better ones—I browsed until something grabbed at me.

"Nope. Never will as long as authors keep writing."

"Dork."

"Perv," I whispered.

"What?"

"You're only here 'cause you wanna sneak a peek. Admit it."

I recognized that energy. Her stupid brother had me tripping the same way last weekend.

"I am not. I'm here for support. You needed the help."

"Yeah, and I've been asking for it all week. As soon as I say he'd be here, you jumped."

"Whatever."

"Mmhm."

Blair was in the bedroom, setting my bed up. I'd slept on only the mattress until now. It reminded me of the old days. Things like headboards didn't matter. We were grateful for a bed to sleep in at all. I never considered us to be poor, but my mom took no one's help. Hell, no one had anything to give. Blair was not as generous back then as he was these days, and my grandmother definitely did what she could. She'd slip me money sometimes.

Blair swore that he'd make up for leaving us hanging when I was younger. Although I was grateful, I felt some type of way about it. I should be used to him spoiling me, but he probably only did it to ease his guilt.

"Your daddy is beyond fine." Janelle admired him from a distance.

"I am so sick of you saying that. Keep it up, I'm telling Cameron."

"Tell him! Ain't nothing wrong with noticing attractive-ness. The crazy thing is how much you look like him."

"So, what? You gonna start leering at me next?"

Janelle threw a book at me. "Ouch, punk."

I walked to my kitchen to get a bottle of water. She followed behind me, searching through my bare pantry.

"Um, where the food at?"

"I haven't shopped yet."

"You been here over two weeks. How you don't have food?"

"Your little fantasy man over there either takes me out to eat or we have dinner at his house with the family. Other times, I have someone bring me cooked food."

"You are so damn spoiled, G!"

I smacked my lips and took a drink.

Nelle smiled. "It looks good on you, though. It's about time some good came your way with everything over the years."

I winced at the thought of "everything." My everything left me one after the other.

"Let's get back to it, okay? In no time we'll be eating at your favorite restaurant on his dime."

"Hey, I can get with that." We walked to the living room to finish setting up books and movies on the shelves. "Still not ready to talk about them, huh?"

"What?"

"You changed the subject, but I won't push. I love you and I know you are still hurting. Gia, you need to talk to someone about it. Get things off your chest."

"You won't push, huh?"

"Okay, okay."

The three of us knocked everything out besides hanging up the decor. I'd do that myself. No way I had enough energy today for it. Blair packed all the empty boxes into his truck, then we were off to stuff our bellies with some over-priced cuisine.

## FOUR

# Gianna

Shana asked me to come by for dinner. Sundays were their family night. They played games, ate plenty of junk, and watched a movie with popcorn. I'd done that with them on a weekday.

Shana insisted that the entire family wanted me to be a part of this tradition. Free food and hanging out with the cutest little brother and sister ever? Of course.

Since Sunday was technically a school night, it began around four in the afternoon. I had nowhere to be. Church ended by noon, so it gave me enough time to chill beforehand if needed.

When I arrived, Olivia jumped into my arms. My heart melted because she got so happy around me. In reality, the festivities couldn't start until I came. She and Jonah were ready to make cookies for the ice cream sandwiches. Shana promised them that dessert, remembering how much I loved them.

Jonah loved cooking about as much as his mother did. He prepared a batch of peanut butter cookies while Liv and

I worked on chocolate chip. Blair and Shana supervised with a glass of wine.

"Put your back into it, Gia. You can mix better than that," Shana noted.

"Keep talking and this batter will fly your way." We chuckled, but the kids had a look on their faces as if I'd get into trouble. "Back me up here. I got your backs." Convincing the kids to add on to the threats was easier than I thought.

"Yeah, Mommy. We got this." Liv scooped up some dough and pretended to flick it.

Blair ducked and almost fell out of the chair, laughing. Jonah tried to do it, too. Shana told them to stop playing with "the mom" look and shut it down.

When the cookies cooled, we sandwiched them with three different ice creams and put them in the freezer. Because cookies and popcorn were on the menu, Shana prepared veggies and dip while we waited on the junk to be ready. I wish my momma would've put some sliced peppers and cauliflower on a plate for my snack.

We prepared personal pizzas as well and then threw them in the oven. Hell, Jonah and Olivia even put veggies on their pizza. I kept it simple with pepperoni and black olives. That was as healthy as my taste buds got.

I laughed so much with Liv attached to me. Having a little sister used to be my dream as a child. That little girl pulled at my heartstrings with every smile, giggle, hug, and kiss on the cheek. Olivia was so kissy, but I loved it.

After playing what seemed like an hour-long Uno game and then Trouble, I was on glass of wine number three. We still had a movie to get through. I felt out of place at moments when I looked at their complete family. Two parents and two kids. Perfect picture. The proof of perfection showed on the kids' innocent little faces.

Once *Fat Albert* started, it reminded me of my childhood being nothing like this. Not that my mom didn't show me an enormous amount of love or that we didn't have fun times together. We had plenty of mommy-daughter days and nights. We had little choice, though.

The kids sat between their parents. I chose the single recliner while they snuggled on the recliner sofa with two bowls of popcorn between them. They even laughed together in perfect unison. It made me sick.

Downing glass number four of wine, my chest tightened as my heart sped up. The lump in my throat was a sign for me to leave. The thoughts running through my mind begged to come out, but this was the worst time to do it. My eyes itched and every blink was in slow motion. I needed water.

"I'll be right back." I reset the recliner to get up and headed to the kitchen. I leaned against the counter, facing the refrigerator. The more deep breaths I took, the more my blood boiled. My hands shook when I reached for the handle to open the fridge.

The water bottles were nestled at the bottom of this big ass refrigerator full of food. Another thing we didn't always have. Momma did her best, and we never went hungry, but there were nights the fridge was bare. Cereal and oatmeal were our go-to if the bills ate up her checks.

I grabbed the water and held it for a minute before finally opening it. What the hell was I doing at this man's house? At that very moment, I realized I'd betrayed my mother. The man who left us hanging all those years gave his other kids everything. Now, I hung out with him as if he'd been a great dad. The memories of feeling lost and unworthy arose. I had to leave.

Before I found my purse and keys, Blair came into the kitchen wearing a smile. "You're missing the movie."

When I faced him, I was on the cusp of tears. "Are you crying?" he whispered.

"I need to go home."

"Why? We're still watching the movie. It's family night. I thought you were okay with that."

I found comfort against the counter again and stared at the man who had a hand in creating me. Something was different this time.

"It's so nice that you have kids worthy enough to get an actual family. Guess I only got your attention after the only real parent I had died."

He tried to step closer, but I put my hand up. "Why are you even trying to be a part of my life now? Do you realize how fucked up that is for you to be all in my face after I buried my mother?"

Blair pointed at me like I was some damn child. "Gia, mind your mouth. I don't want your sister and brother to hear you speak that way."

"Oh, yeah, your precious angels. Guess I wasn't as precious at that age. I had to grow up knowing my father didn't give two shits about me. Had another family that didn't work out. Got married again to start over. What happens when shit falls apart with Shana? You're gonna act like Liv and Jonah don't exist and start over with another woman?"

My tears failed to stay at bay at the thought of sweet Liv hurt because her dad abandoned her. I knew the feeling all too well, but she'd experienced his love from the start. All I had was the hope of what he'd be like. I had no clue until I became an adult.

My mom avoided talking about Blair and I understood

why. Who wanted to praise a man that walked out? Hell, he was never with her in the first place since he got married so soon after. No way he didn't play my mom back then until she got pregnant.

"Gia, I think you had a little too much wine. You are not making any sense. I'm not that type of man. I'm here because I love you."

"Hmph! And when did you realize that? Once the woman you tricked to think you cared and whose heart you ripped out was no longer here to stop you from hurting her only daughter? She said you'd disappoint me because that was all you knew how to do."

"How am I doing that now? I thought you were happy."

"Happy? My fucking mother is dead. Where's the happiness in that? And now you throw your perfect little family in my face. You don't want anything to do with me. You just want to prove to yourself that you aren't as bad as my mother said. Happy." I chuckled. "This guy."

Shana entered the kitchen. "Is everything okay? Gia?" She ripped off a paper towel and handed it to me to wipe my face. "Gia, what's the matter?"

Shana had nothing to do with this. Wife number two had shown me so much love. I didn't want to hurt her sensitive ass feelings. She looked like she wanted to cry for no reason.

"Nothing at all. It's just time for me to go home."

"No! You cannot drive in this condition," Blair blurted out.

"Condition?" Shana stepped closer. "What's going on?"

Blair motioned his hand my way. "She's drunk."

"Aht! I'm not drunk. I'm tipsy. There's a difference. It did nothing but give me clarity on who my father really is, and I was only telling him about it. He doesn't agree so now I'm supposedly drunk."

Shana leaned on the refrigerator opposite me. "Well, even if you are tipsy, you shouldn't operate a vehicle of any kind."

"Ugh, not you too?" I rolled my eyes at her after she tilted her head like what she said was final.

"I want to make sure you are safe. Let's be on the cautious side and I'll get the guest room ready for you."

"Shana, thank you. I am fine and I have to go to work in the morning."

Blair stood next to his wife. "Let us take you home. I'll drive your car and you can ride with Shana and the kids. How does that sound?"

"It sounds like something I don't want to do. We shouldn't drag your worthy angels out at night for your worthless, drunk daughter to get home. I mean tipsy. Just tipsy."

He blew out air. "That is not at all true. I love you."

"Is that your heart or your guilty conscience talking? Your love came twenty years too late."

Shana placed her left hand on Blair's arm and the right one across her chest. "Okay, that's... Honey, leave us, please?"

Blair shook his head. "I won't. She cannot leave like this."

"I agree, and I will take care of her. Go check on the kids."

"Yeah, go." I waved his way to dismiss him. He hesitated and planted his eyes right on mine. "Bye, my loving father."

"Gia, stop. I do love you. I should have never let—"

"Blair!" Shana raised her voice. "Leave us. I got it."

After he let out what felt like a five-minute-long ass

breath, he walked away. Shana grabbed both my hands and held them tight. She gazed at me like she knew me. She didn't. Not that much. The sorrow in her eyes was enough to push me over the edge.

My body shuddered, with more tears pouring. Shana wrapped her arms around me. I sank into her embrace as if my own mother held me, and I cried like a baby.

Why did she even care? What was she doing holding me? I didn't belong to her. She couldn't understand me. Yet, it seemed like she did. Shana squeezed at the right moments as if this wasn't the first time we'd done this.

"Let it out, Gia. You're hurting. Let it out."

I fought like hell not to do any of that, but my damn emotions listened to her. I wanted my mom. I wanted Mimi. Not Blair. He wasn't there when it had mattered the most, but somehow he was the only blood I had left. That shit wasn't fair on any planet.

# FIVE

# Gianna

SHANA WOKE ME UP AT FIVE IN THE MORNING. SHE asked if I wanted her to make me breakfast before I left. I declined, freshened up, then met her in the kitchen.

No one else roamed the house at this hour. Blair had left for work already. Something about a long day he'd have went in one ear and out the other. I didn't want to talk about him. I thanked her for not getting upset with my behavior the night before.

Once I cried every drop I had last night, Shana convinced me to stay and that she'd make sure I got up in time to get home before work. We talked a bit once she somewhat tucked me in. Shana had pretty much married her father. What I'd gone through with Blair, she'd experienced with her dad. As much as I wanted to act like she'd never get it, she did.

Embarrassment was the least of my problems. Blair took everything hard, according to Shana. I said things that got to him, causing him to lose sleep before whatever important day this was for his job. It legitimately wasn't my intention.

When I agreed to join their family night, my intention

was to be a part of the family in a positive capacity. I blamed the wine, but deep down, everything I spewed was my true feelings.

We said goodbye after she invited me to come to her to unload whenever necessary. She even offered to refer me to her therapist because she still dealt with issues from her childhood beyond what she'd shared with me. It wouldn't be the first time someone claimed therapy could help me. I wasn't even against it. I didn't think I was ready to talk about my feelings yet.

On my way home, I listened to Mimi's favorite genre: gospel. I needed a little Jesus music to redeem my ugliness. Even if I'd meant it, that wasn't the way or the time to present it.

I made it home in time for a long shower and a quick breakfast. The more I sat alone, the more I figured I should apologize to Blair. It'd happen eventually. An honest sit down between the two of us would be the ideal setting. I'd make that happen sometime soon. For now, I had to get my ass to work.

---

I walked out of my building after work, ready for a drink or five. Something had to erase last night from my mind. Ignoring the problem used to work well for me, but this thing with Blair hit differently. Only one person could distract me the way I wanted, but it was too early for a booty call. Instead, I thought of my boo and called her.

Janelle couldn't meet me anywhere. She had plans already. I didn't want to drink at home. So, I searched for some place that had good food and good liquor. I'd get myself a table and watch TV discreetly on my phone with headphones on. Luckily, having company was never a requirement for me to have a good time outside the house.

I remembered Janelle telling me about a seafood joint that she fell in love with. I asked her about it and she texted me the basic details. Unfortunately, the restaurant didn't serve a wide variety of liquor. I'd settle for a stop at a liquor store after picking up the food. My balcony still counted as going out since it was outside.

I almost drooled at the aroma before I got out of my car in the Lotus Seafood parking lot. No way this place would let me down. Still, disappointment was precisely what I found when I reached the door.

"Eve?" D'Mario's eyes widened like I caught him doing something wrong since a woman was attached to his arm.

"Excuse me? You're mistaken." I tried to play it off. Rule number one was that we didn't speak outside of the hotel room.

"You don't have to worry about her. She's not my girl like that," he barely whispered.

"I don't really care. You still don't know me. Remember that next time, okay?"

"Damn, girl. I thought you were only mean after sex."

I pressed my lips together hard to stop myself from cussing this supposed-to-be stranger out. Well, he was indeed a stranger. Just one I'd done nasty things with.

"You live around here?"

"Nope," I let out, with no hesitation. Even if I did, he would not find out.

The woman who stood a few inches taller than me slightly bumped his shoulder. I guess she wasn't for this run-in. Hell, neither was I. I told him he had the wrong person and carried on about my business.

The line was long enough for me to decide what I

wanted and wait in anticipation for what might be the best seafood to please my palate. With one person in front of me, some dude bum-rushed past and skipped me. I pushed his back.

"Are you crazy? You see me standing here." When he turned around, I wished that push was a punch upside the head. "Zak, what the hell? Why are you here?"

"For the same reason you are. I'm hungry."

"Your hungry ass can get in the back of the line. Move!"

"Come on, the game is coming on soon. You being here was a sign that I might make it back home before it starts."

"Zak, if you don't get yo' ass—"

"I'll pay for yours too."

I scrunched my face. "Fine, I'm ordering the most expensive thing then."

He shrugged his shoulders, bringing my attitude to the forefront. Hell, it didn't have time to rest after seeing D'Mario. Zak had a way of making me want to slap him on sight. Lately, he'd been too present in my space and thoughts. "Why do I keep running into you?"

"'Cause you want to." He winked at me over his shoulder, then continued typing on his phone. "The law of attraction."

"Boy, please." It was our turn. My turn. The cashier asked what we wanted. Zak immediately answered for himself. "Get me that." I pointed to a picture of snow crab and shrimp. "I also want hush puppies and some Louisiana fried rice."

"You want the whole kitchen to go with that?" He paused while pulling his wallet from his pocket.

"That's the price of skipping, little boy."

"You lucky I got it."

"No, *you* lucky."

He paid for the food and we stood on the side of the counter to wait for it. There weren't any seats available. "I should've ordered over the phone."

"Is it always like this?" I asked for lack of anything else to talk about.

"What?"

"This crowded."

"Depends on when you come. Sometimes I catch them at the perfect time with no line."

"Your sister swears by this place."

"It is good." Zak stared at me too long for comfort. "Where you eating at?"

"Why?" I shrugged and rolled my neck.

He smacked his lips. "Why do you always ask why?"

I laughed at my defensive habit and shrugged. "Probably because I don't like nosy people."

"Same old attitude."

"Same old asshole."

"An asshole who's buying your dinner."

"No, you bought a spot in the line."

"Keep talking and I will run outta here with all the food. Then whatchu gonna do?"

"Wanna find out?"

He narrowed his eyes and scrunched his face in the cutest damn way. How could he make that expression cute? "Maybe."

A girl called Zak's name. He took the bags from the cashier, then that fool got into a running stance, holding the bag like a damn football.

I grabbed his arm with both hands. The strength in one could probably lift me up with ease. I swallowed hard to get the thought of his arms holding me in the air, doing things I'd never do with him. "You'd better not. Don't play."

That smile flashed, making my damn panties catch a drip. This was not happening. Not even in my thoughts. I didn't care how fine Zak's stupid butt had gotten. He was off-limits for more reasons than one.

I followed him outside, waiting for him to give me my food. "I don't have time to sort this. Come to my place and I will drop you off after the game."

"Hell, no. Give me my food. It won't take more than thirty seconds. Stop playing with me. I'm hungry."

"G, for real. It's about to start and I only have enough time to get home."

He couldn't be serious. Before I could answer, he took off to his car with me in tow and put the bags in the backseat. "Get in."

"Zak, for real? Why? My car is right there. Just give me my food." There was one car between us.

"Aight, I'm leaving without you." He got in and turned the car on.

"I fucking hate you right now."

"That ain't news."

I got in my car and followed him. Zak's apartment was less than ten minutes away. I almost fell behind with him power-walking from the parking lot. He stayed on the third floor and flew up the damn stairs like a maniac. I took my time because I'd be damned if I tripped and fell on concrete stairs.

He opened the door to his place and set the food on the coffee table. Zak walked to his kitchen and returned with two beers. He stopped rushing once he came from his room without shoes.

"Okay, you made it. What the hell were you trying to watch?"

Zak plopped onto the couch beside me. I finally opened

the bags to get to the food, finding mine on the first attempt. "A show on Netflix. People say it's crazy."

"I know gotdamn well you're joking," I borderline yelled.

He got up and howled all over the living room. "Zak, do not stand there and tell me you dragged me over here for nothing."

"Of course, not for nothing. The prize is all over your face right now."

I hopped off the couch and swung at him. The first time I missed, but not the second. I caught him in the chest. "Ouch." He palmed my fist after another attempt to pop him. My free hand missed too. He held both my fists, leaving me no choice but to kick. "Ay, girl. Calm down."

"What is wrong with you?" He let go of me, laughing all over again. "You are so stupid. I could be home by now."

"Tell that to that long ass line at Lotus. I had to take advantage of your spot."

"So, your stupid ass lied. Why did you have to bring me here?"

"Like you had something better to do."

"I did. Eat in peace."

"You can do that here."

"Minus your dumb ass."

"Sit down and eat. Now I don't have to watch this show alone." He sat down and took everything from the bags.

"You were serious about that?"

"Yeah." Zak picked up the remote and navigated to Netflix.

From the looks of his recommendations, we watched the same type of stuff. "I hope I already saw it so I can spoil it for you."

"Just mean for no reason." He bumped my shoulder with his.

"Oh, you gave me a reason tonight."

He stopped searching on the TV and opened his box of food. "A'ight, maybe I did. You can chill with an old friend, right?"

My head whipped to the left and right. "Where he at?"

"Funny."

I dug in on the snow crab as soon as I opened my container. After inhaling one leg, I tried the fried rice with some sauce drizzled on top as Zakari suggested. What they called "crack sauce" did me in, and there was no turning back.

Zak put on *Another Life*, and we watched the first three episodes before it got too late. We kept laughing even though the show was far from comedy. That fool talked to the screen as much as I did. I never did it in public, but hell, he made it seem normal. All that suspense and borderline horror had us both on the edge of our seats. His reactions were too similar to mine that I cracked up each time we almost said the same thing.

No one would ever find out, but I actually had a good time with his big head ass.

---

"So, my brother didn't leave you hanging last night?" Janelle called me during my commute home. My favorite way to ride home at the worst hour was listening to a good book. A nasty one was even better. These authors today be getting people pregnant for real. I had to save the next chapter for the morning.

"Who told you that?"

"Puh-lease! Any interaction Zak has with you will always reach my ears. Plus, I told him to meet you there. I felt bad about not being available since you lonely in these streets."

"Heifer, I ain't lonely. What if I didn't go?"

"You were asking too many damn questions about the place not to. If you didn't show up, he would've gotten the hint. No harm done. It's only Zak."

"So, let me get this straight. You had your little brother stake out Lotus in case I showed up, so I wouldn't be alone?"

"You make it sound pathetic."

"No, *you* made *me* sound pathetic. Hell, you should've let me think it was a chance encounter."

Her laugh burst through my car's speakers. "What? He had no plans for the night either. I didn't want you to eat alone."

"I've been eating alone just fine for years, Nelle. You got me looking like I ain't got no friends. In front of his dumb ass at that."

"Zak ain't worried about that, so stop. And, uh, where your other friends at? 'Cause I ain't seen none of 'em."

"Oh, shut up."

My friends were six feet under the ground at Paradise Cemetery. Mimi and Momma. Janelle was the only one I got close to as a kid. We talked to people in school but not close enough to keep in touch past a few Facebook likes.

The rest of my clan lived near Miami. Nelle had a point, but I didn't need Zak knowing my business nor did I need his pity company. All of it negated the fact that I had a good time with him. He was probably decent because his sister had asked him to be.

"Your brother wasn't a bad distraction from my depressing loneliness," I dragged out the word depressing.

"Be quiet. That's not what I think."

"Sure it isn't."

"I'm glad he didn't completely piss you off or run you away. His hoe ass acts like he can't spend time around women unless he was sleeping with them. I get that he's young, but it's disappointing. Our parents instilled in him to respect women."

As much as we called him a youngin', Zak was only a few months younger than me. Janelle was barely a year older. Nelle was born in October, and her mother got pregnant months later. Zak's birthday was the following December, making him right behind us in school. Then he failed the eighth grade, keeping him yet another year back. Zak and I were born the same year, but I was a summer baby.

We called him young to his face to piss him off. Any other time she said it was weird since we were all basically the same age.

"Like you said, he's young. We all are."

"He's still stupid. I hope he doesn't knock one of his females up like most of the guys he used to hang out with. They are some poor girl's baby's daddy."

"Let the boy live."

"I do. I haven't met not one girl he's been with. Not a one. I've heard so many names, but never seen a face. Not even on social media."

"Why you so bothered by it?"

"Because I had higher hopes for him. With Mom and Dad as good examples, I never thought he'd become *that* guy."

"The boy is the same age as me. Hell, you aren't too much older. Life is short. Whatever makes a person happy is their right."

"Why are you even defending him? I thought you hated him."

"Understanding that part of him doesn't mean I don't. He still gets on my nerves like always, but you can't expect everyone to have the same ideals with relationships. It's not for everybody."

"You sound like you're speaking from experience. Is that why you never want to be in one?"

I smacked my lips because this was a broken record. Not something to rehash.

Janelle sighed into the phone. "Fine. I will lay off, but I think you're being ridiculous with this whole family curse thing. You gave no one a chance."

"Yeah, well, it hasn't failed me yet. No risks, no pain. I'm good."

"Sure you are."

"Whatever, J. I gotta go."

"Guess I'm pissing you off again. Good thing you don't live far. You can't avoid me for weeks like you did in Miami."

She hung up before letting me get my last word in. Janelle knew how much I hated that shit. The truth might've been in what she said, but it didn't mean she could throw it around like I was a bad person.

Things weren't so easy after losing the most important people in my life. Janelle was the type who claimed to understand my problems but threw it in my face when it served her. That was definitely one thing I hadn't missed.

SIX

# Zakari

Myesha hit me up last night when Gia came over. We'd been at it for a little over two months. She had beef with her daughter's father, who I played ball with a time or two at the Y. Girlie jacked me up in the restroom after one of our games. She walked straight up in there, telling me what she wanted me to do to her.

At first, I wasn't with that shit. The way she came at me was a turnoff. Myesha was nothing less than persistent. I'd see her on days I worked out. She'd be alone and try to entice me with that fat ass in yoga pants. After asking what her deal was, she broke down about being mistreated and only wanting to feel good. Her one promise was that she wouldn't tell her man. She saw me, wanted me, and came after me.

Dammit if she wasn't down for whatever. Myesha had hungry eyes every time we met up. Never a dull moment. But I wasn't a fool. When we met up, I'd get a hotel with rooms only accessible through the lobby. I wasn't about to have her man running up on me at my apartment if he ever found out what his girl did behind his back.

I hadn't seen her in a week. She was the type who needed a fix every few days. Her call would've been right on time any other day.

My sister had begged me to make time for Gia early yesterday evening. Janelle didn't have to ask twice. She mentioned something about how much Gia needed a friend because of some drama with her dad.

The most I'd learned about the dude was that he was some doctor, never around for Gia as a kid and that Janelle crushed on his old ass. I'd seen him two or three times. Anyone who put Gia in so much pain was trash in my book.

I remembered back when she used to tell Janelle how much she envied our family because we had both parents. As much trouble as I gave Gia, that part made me feel bad for her. When Janelle mentioned Gia having recent issues with the man, I had to be there for her somehow, even if she was unaware of the fact.

Earlier today, I got a call from my boy, Byron. Since high school, we'd been running together. He got cuffed last year by a woman we met at Berryhill restaurant. We'd frequented the restaurant for years with about four other dudes who'd all drifted away the year before last.

It used to be our spot until one karaoke night. We only showed up to laugh at the fools that got up to embarrass themselves. Trina walked through the doors with her group of friends and dude fell hard.

My brother drank the Kool-Aid, making it his mission to get me to down a cup. That was a hard pass for me. The way he fell for Trina was one for the books. I couldn't get a hold of him for weeks. When he finally came up for air, he'd always showed up with her. It forced me to make new friends until my boy could find a little piece of himself again.

We met up at Top Golf for a game or two. We had to do the most when we hung out because he didn't get out as much. It got better from the beginning of their relationship, but seeing him in person still seemed like a rare occasion.

I made a big deal about it when we found each other inside, embarrassing him.

"You one ignant nigga, for real." He laughed at my display of affection, giving him the most ostentatious dap and praising him for breaking away from his regular programming to see an old friend.

We got on the list to play. The wait gave us a chance to have a drink and catch up.

"Trina still got you on a tight ass leash, man. I ain't seen you in years."

"Man, shut up. I saw you last month."

"Nigga, we used to hang out multiple times a week. I think I'm having withdrawals."

Byron chuckled. "You can stop that shit right there. My lady had nothing to do with that. You cut that time laying under a hundred females."

"Nah. Nothing like that."

"You did. We'd try to go somewhere and then you'd call to cancel 'cause some shorty hit you up."

I shook my head. "I don't remember that shit."

"Of course you don't. Trina came at the perfect time to save me from being neglected."

We chuckled at that. Byron ran through more girls than I did before his lady changed him.

In high school, we'd started smelling ourselves once the females did. College stepped it up a bit. Even as freshmen, we'd had our share of closed-book study sessions. Being roommates all four years turned us into savages back then.

The Take Her Down brothers had one goal. No girlfriends. Only female friends who wanted a taste of the THD brothers. The girls back then were wild. My first threesome happened on campus with girls claiming to be best friends. It was crazy, but I loved it.

Deep down, we accepted that life in the fast lane wouldn't last forever, so we took advantage of good looks and spending more free time in the gym than playing video games. Ladies loved a man with a powerful physique. We had a disciplined workout regimen for a good six years. Then I was on my own. He'd rather go with his girl.

"If anyone got neglected, it's me."

Byron twisted his mouth. "So, you been sitting around the house waiting on me?"

"Now you know me better than that. You still my brother."

"I am. Always will be."

"How's Trina? Since she's all you care about these days."

"Man, chill. My lady is good."

"Cool. I'm happy for you."

"You need to get with the program and find you a good one, so I can ask you the same thing. I want to be happy for you too."

"Who said I wasn't? I got plenty options to keep me satisfied on any given night."

"Man, I mean the real shit. The kind of thing that makes you think about the future."

"I ain't tryna hear that bullshit, B. My future is mine and mine alone. I got shit to do."

"You can still do what you need to and have a queen holding you down. The right one makes you better, man."

"I ain't seen you in forever and probably will take

another few months until the next time. Can't you think of something else to talk about?"

"I'm only looking out. I don't want to see you caught up with a female you can't stand like Dino and Greg. Both got a kid with a woman they don't get along with all because they were living the life you can't seem to let go of."

"You talking like we hitting forty. Let me at least turn thirty before we even think about heading down this boring ass road. And I ain't them niggas. I protect myself."

Byron shrugged me off. He acted like he was some damn love recruiter. Everybody wanted you to have what they had when they thought they were happy. But everybody's happiness didn't look the same.

"Don't you want more?" he asked.

"Man, come on."

"Zak, for real."

I dropped my head back and waved for him to finish. Hopefully, he'd get all this shit out before our game.

"You don't want to be this way forever, do you? There's so much more than sex with different women."

"Enlighten me. What do I have to look forward to?"

"Dates in public. Vacations. Legit knowing a person inside and out and loving them anyway. Talking and sharing."

"Man, you sound real weak right now."

"You sound dumb as hell. This shit you doing with these females ain't gonna last. You will get tired of it. By then, the woman for you will be with someone who was willing to grow up when you wouldn't."

"A'ight, enough of that. I'm good. I got time. Right now, I'm living my best life." I tried to mimic Lil Duval.

"You a fool."

"At least I still got control of my mind. I swear you

sound like my sister and any other female who wants me to settle down with them. Y'all are the ones doing the shit wrong. You think you found the right person when you barely know yourself. Ten years in, y'all are the same motherfuckers who will be divorced, fighting for shared custody. I don't want that shit. Let me take my time and understand myself first. I'm still in my twenties. Not in my forties or even thirties. I'm doing exactly what a nigga my age should be doing."

"Yeah, and what's that?"

"Living my best life." I nailed the imitation that time.

Byron laughed so hard; he choked a bit on the drink he'd just taken.

I heard what he said, but that woman hadn't crossed paths with me. Only one had me wanting all that he mentioned in imagination only. Crushing on Gia as a youngin' stayed with me for a while because she was always around. In college, she didn't come up much. Now that she'd moved back? It crossed my mind a few times.

The woman had everything a man could want. Sexy as fuck, intelligent, and crazy enough, her smart ass mouth. She got at me whenever I came at her wrong. That shit turned me on like a motherfucker. Thinking about her was one thing. Seeing her did some crazy shit to me.

Gia had gotten thicker since two years ago when I'd seen her at her grandmother's funeral. Because of the circumstances, I shouldn't have been looking at her then. With our history, I couldn't look away. I wanted to hold her and comfort her, wishing I could take the pain away. Soft shit.

Her ass, though? A feature that proved she, in fact, could get sexier. Gia's hair was shorter back then. That tiny waist opened up to hips that I imagined grabbing onto. I took all that sexual frustration out on a few women for a while before their own faces were enough. Gia's face was all I had imagined after she left.

Now, she'd somehow put on some weight in all the right places. Gia was thin growing up. Now? Those thick thighs and almost slim waist took me back to that little boy, wishing she'd be mine one day. As a grown-ass man, those same thoughts ran through my mind.

Last night did nothing but escalate it. I had to convince myself not to call one of my ladies up to pretend to be with Gia. None of them came close to the level of sexiness she commanded without even trying.

Byron knew all about my feelings for Gia as a teen. I wondered if he remembered her. Bringing her up would hurt my case of only wanting to be free because I'd give all this shit up if she ever looked at me as more than Janelle's little brother. That wasn't in the cards for me, though.

We finally got our turn after our second beer. I whooped his ass, even though we both did terribly. Byron laid off the Kool-Aid talk and we walked down memory lane with each swing. Damn, we had some good times. All that changed because that nigga fell in love.

If I ever found that special someone, I'd still remember myself. That part of his perfect life with Trina wasn't appealing. I wanted a woman who'd allow me to be the man I was. Not one to change me to the point where my friends didn't recognize me.

# SEVEN

## Gianna

A LITTLE OVER A MONTH BACK IN TOWN, THE reminder of the second worst day in my history consumed me. The anniversary of my grandmother's passing. Mimi transitioned peacefully in her sleep at eighty-two. She had so much life and energy for her age, I'd never imagined she'd give out so soon.

The last time I saw her was on a cruise. It was something neither of us had ever done. That woman drove me crazy that week.

Our trip on the grand cruise ship took us to Jamaica. Mimi kept inquiring about that herbal remedy usually wrapped in paper. Those people probably thought she was a crazy old lady.

One guy hooked us up and I got high with my grandmother. It was the best trip of my life and I wished I could relive it right now with her.

In her enhanced mindfulness, she kept saying things about being tired and ready to see my mom again. I chalked it up to the weed, but she meant it. She repeatedly told me how much she loved me and how she wished I'd come out of my ways and find a nice man to settle down with.

I objected to the idea because of the track record of past generations. Her dad had dipped on her mother too. Nothing convinced me the same wouldn't happen to me. So, no love, no relationships, no babies.

Mimi sang a different tune later in her life. As a kid, she was on Momma's side, convincing me that good men didn't mesh with my family. Generations of single mothers each having one daughter made them feel we were somehow cursed. I believed it.

I was grateful this day fell on the weekend. Janelle called early to check on me, so it came as no surprise that she knocked on the door.

"I have Fireball and greasy food menus saved on my phone."

I hugged her as tightly as possible. "You always come through for me."

"Hey, we don't get to be friends this long and I don't learn your ways. That 'I just want to be alone' crap doesn't work on me."

"That's why I love you."

"Love you too, boo!"

Janelle grabbed two glasses from the cabinet and added ice to them. "It's not cold, so ice will have to do the first round." After pouring a decent amount, she put the bottle in the freezer.

In times like these, I was glad we'd stayed close when I moved to Florida to go to the University of Miami. We could've easily lost touch with each other with the distance and the fact that both of us dealt with busy ass schedules in school.

Momma had somehow became a huge college football

fan and had a soft spot for the U. I experienced the school, the city, and her beloved football games for myself. Although, I hated sports, I learned to love the school spirit.

I'd send my mom pictures or videos of my view of the field in hopes she'd get the guts to visit for a game. She feared planes and hated missing work even more. Working in a nursing home, she rarely wanted to leave her patients. If they had little time left, she wanted to be there for them since many didn't have any family visiting.

For sophomore year, Blair flew Janelle to visit me many weekends. We'd do the things I wanted to do with Momma. Being in that stadium made me feel closer to my mom.

After college, I stayed in Miami after accepting an internship that turned into a permanent position. Mimi hated that I'd made that choice, but she got the chance to visit the dope-ass city often. We burned on the beach each time she visited.

Mimi never got over being able to see her feet in the water. Growing up with only Surfside and Galveston, any shade of water besides brown was something to see. After she passed away, every time I chilled at the beach, I had another thing to cry about.

Janelle ordered Chinese food while I picked the movie lineup for the day. I wanted to watch Mimi's top five movies that I grew to love myself. *The Color Purple, Mahogany, Lady Sings the Blues, Sparkle,* and *The Five Heartbeats.* After the second movie, we had ordered wings.

Zakari called Janelle and brought beer and everything needed for margaritas. To my surprise, he was very mature and supportive.

After walking to the couch where I planted myself, his unforgivably sexy ass leaned down and squeezed me in his arms. It felt way too good.

"I'm sorry you going through this, man. I remember how close you two were." Zak offered a sympathetic smile that felt like another warm embrace.

"Thank you, Zak. I appreciate it." A quick chuckle escaped me. "Who woulda guessed you had a nice bone in your body."

"Ay, don't be like that. This is serious. Besides, you're family. I always wanted a big brother. You stepped right into that role." I tried to kick him but missed and didn't possess enough energy to chase him when he took off to the kitchen howling.

I tried to hold my laugh in. "I fucking hate you."

Janelle popped him for me. He made our drinks with her help. Seeing those two did so much for my spirit.

As much as Zak remained an asshole, I was happy to have my true family with me. The girls in Miami didn't get to see me like this. These two were there throughout it all. So, by default, they knew the side of me.

Two years ago, Janelle had called me with the devastating news. Mimi and I called each other every morning and every night. It gave us a designated time to talk and unload if needed. She was my heart and I told her almost everything.

Mimi didn't answer one morning, but I called an hour later in case she'd missed the first. After still no word, I asked Janelle to swing by, hoping Mimi's phone got silenced accidentally. Each minute in suspense felt like my oxygen levels decreased. Then the call came that my worse fear had become my living nightmare.

I took a week off from work to go home after making all the arrangements. Really, Shana did most of them. I zoned out until we put Mimi in the ground. My body gave out after they lowered hers. I collapsed to the ground and wouldn't allow anyone to touch me. Janelle sat with me and Zak waited for us. He waited for over an hour after everyone left because I couldn't move.

The repast was held at my grandmother's house with her friends. Blair, Shana, and the kids attended without me. I hadn't planned on missing it, but I'd hated the first one I went to and couldn't will myself to do it again.

Instead, Janelle took me to her place to sleep the day away. Nothing else had to be done. Thanks to a packing and moving company Blair had hired, everything I'd keep was moved to a storage unit. The key to her belongings was on my key ring, but I hadn't been there yet.

I sat on the couch, remembering Mimi's favorite parts in the original *Sparkle*. She didn't hate the remake because Whitney was her girl, but Irene Cara would be the only Sparkle in her heart. I sang every song like we used to. That part when Sister died took me out for a few minutes. Out of all the deaths in our movie lineup, seeing that woman in the casket was the last straw. It could've been the drinking, but that scene felt like deep stabs.

Zak scooted closer to me and pulled me into his shoulder. "Come on, G. Men ain't supposed to cry."

I punched him like six times in the arm. "You get on my nerves."

Both of their laughs cheered me up again. "I see you tryna get a feel with all those love taps."

"Keep playing, I'm going for your nuts."

My fist got close enough for him to flinch. "Ay, quit playing. I want kids one day. We know you don't, so play with your own sack."

He picked up his beer and I tipped it over fast. Only a little came out. "Why you gotta be childish?"

"Look at you two. Get a room already," Janelle spat out on her way to the fridge.

I smacked my lips. "Oh, both of y'all asses are crazy."

Zak raised his index finger for Janelle's attention. "I'm only into women." He laughed so hard when I tried to attack him. I got him upside the head a few times before he grabbed my hands and overpowered me.

"Why you getting so mad? I'm playing. I—" His phone chirped. He pushed me over with ease and checked it. "Oh, shit! Gotta go."

"Let me guess. Thot duty?" I rolled my eyes.

Zak's smirk made me regret asking. "Don't be jealous. I got a few you can hit up if you really lonely."

I jumped up from my spot, ready to slap him, but he wrapped his arms around me first. "I got love for you, G. Call me if you need anything. I got you." He kissed my temple and made it all weird, holding me for too long. My ass took a whiff of him, closing my eyes. When comfort tried to settle in, I jerked myself away.

Zak looked into my eyes, making me quickly avoid his. He cleared his throat, dapped me up, and walked over to Janelle. A minute later, it was just the girls again.

"You can go too if you need to. I'm okay now. Cameron probably misses that—"

"Aht! Don't even say it. He knows where I'm at. And where I will be until tomorrow. You ain't getting rid of me tonight, so stop trying."

"Aww! You really love me." I nudged her arm when she got comfortable next to me on the couch.

"Like that's ever going to change. Family first."

"Family first." I finished my watery margarita before guzzling down the bottle of water she handed me.

Janelle's big brown eyes were glued to the side of my face. "Nelle, would you say it already?"

"Nope, I want you to say it. 'Cause you already know."

"What? That you are still certifiable."

"No. I'm talking about how much Zak is—"

"Anyway!" I yelled over her. "It's time for the last movie." I got up to put in *The Five Heartbeats*.

It didn't matter what she had to say. We weren't going there today. That boy was not on my mind. Not his beautiful white teeth, juicy lips, or any parts of him covered in that black t-shirt and fitted, ripped jeans. Fitted enough for me to know his thighs were of power and glory, with heaven most likely between them. Ain't nobody thinking about none of that.

"I'ma leave it alone for now, but I see yo' ass, G."

"Then stop looking." She chuckled and so did I. My stomach felt empty yet again.

I rubbed my belly. "I think I want some sushi."

"You greedy, but I'm down. Oooh, we should make funnel cakes. I saw the pancake mix in the fridge."

I nodded. "Sounds like a plan."

"Cool. This is fun! I mean, not the reason behind it, obviously. I missed this. Junk food and movies. Mimi would've been chilling right along with us."

"Downing a bottle before we finished one drink."

We laughed at the memories of her falling asleep with her mouth open when she drank too much. Mimi thought she could hang, claiming to have been drinking longer than we'd been breathing.

I wished she was here.

# EIGHT

# Gianna

I scheduled a quick recovery session for my temporary depression.

"You made it." D'Mario's smile and lowered lids had me ready. He backed away, opening the door wider for me to walk in. I tossed my purse on the chair.

D'Mario wore nothing but sweatpants. That meant he understood what this was this time around. I wouldn't have to argue with his ass when I wanted to leave.

"And you look...like you're happy to see me." I locked my eyes on the goods. Damn, if this man didn't look like a whole meal, fuck a snack.

D'Mario laughed and made his way to me. "Let me show you." Those long arms wrapped around my waist. One hand moved to the small of my back and the other to the back of my neck.

He came in too close to my face. "No kissing. I told you—"

"Shh, I remember your damn rules." He pulled me in tighter and kissed my neck instead. As long as his lips stayed away from mine, we good. The men I sexed were available to other women, so lips were off-limits. I didn't know where they'd been. If I smelled another woman on them, our deal was off for the night. Not for jealousy, but because they didn't wash their ass or face. Protection wasn't enough at that point.

While D'Mario nibbled on my neck and shoulders, I inhaled him. He passed. No funk from earlier sex sessions I knew he put on other women. With his smooth, dark brown skin, ripped body, and sexy ass smile, he got plenty. His attitude told me so. He knew what he was doing.

All the kissing got on my nerves, though. I didn't need it. I came for one thing, and it wasn't his lips. I placed my hands on each of his pecs and pushed him off. He barely stumbled backward and dropped his head in a smirk. "I see you getting impatient again."

"'Cause you stalling. Take your clothes off." I gave him directions as I followed the same, removing everything from my body. When we were both in the same suit, that thang retook my attention. It almost dazed me until I remembered how it felt inside me the last time. I snapped out of the memory of it to get the real thing.

"Damn, you so sexy, Eve." I pushed him down onto the bed and waited for him to put on that extra layer to protect both of us. When he finished, I tried to straddle him. He gently placed his hand on my neck to stop me. "Let me taste you."

"No, I want to feel you." Oral sex wasn't part of the deal either because I had no intention of reciprocating. All I wanted was within grasp, but he kept denying me.

D'Mario picked me up and put me on my back. "Trust me, you will. Relax." Before I had a chance to contest, his finger forced moans from me. "Now, that's what I'm talking about." His thick fingers invaded my love pocket, hooking on the inside. He pushed two inside me while his thumb made circles around my bean. The arch in my back as his rhythm increased put a smile on his face. "Yeah, that's it, Eve. Relax, baby."

I conceded and closed my eyes. Then the tip of D'Mario's tongue trailed along my inner thigh before it relieved his fingers. He gripped both my thighs, spreading them wide.

The warmth of his mouth on me shot straight up my spine. I didn't want this, but it felt so damn good. The smacking of his lips against my lower ones drew more moisture from me. "You taste better than I imagined." The breath of his words on me made me shudder.

"Shit, D'Mario." I wasn't going out like that. My hardness softened with each lick, each bite, each suck. I hated this kind of shit. I failed to stay in control with a man's tongue lashing at my love.

I tried to release his grip, but he wouldn't let go. He locked my thighs down and covered me from my clit to the tip of my perineum. My body stiffened, trying to hold back, but it was already too late. Moans graduated to screams as I hit the point of no return. He had me.

D'Mario tugged at my bean with his teeth after licking me clean of my love water. "You sound so sexy." His tongue had my ass moaning and squirming even after he came up. I didn't enjoy being this damn vulnerable. He'd pay for that shit.

I punched his chest. He laughed. "What's that for? That good, huh?" His smirk made me giggle. I pushed him down on his back and grabbed his rock-hard dick to stroke. His head fell back and his eyes closed. That smirk faded quickly.

I squeezed it but was careful around the tip. After a

minute of muffled moans from my hand job, I straddled him and sat on the tip, gripping him with my walls the whole way down. "Fuck, girl!" D'Mario's eyes squeezed shut until I came all the way down on it.

My mouth watered at him filling me up to the brim. He had a dream dick. The perfect size, but almost too much. That perfect balance between pleasure and pain. I winced when it hit too deep, but kept going because it was worth it. Even though it didn't belong to me, at the moment, none of that mattered. I claimed it for the night and took all of him like I was trying to keep him.

D'Mario held onto my hips as I rode him like I had something to prove. When I hit the right spot, I rode that shit out until I came, then I switched it up. He sat up, trying to slow my movements. His strength turned me on even more. "Slow down, baby. I ain't tryna come right now. Hold on, a'ight." The slow strides facing him were dangerous for me. That man looked into my eyes, biting his bottom lip, tempting me to bite it too. *No kissing!*

Another orgasm broke my attention from him. I pushed him back down and rode him backward. "Ah, shit! Shit!" He helped me ride him slowly and that alone almost knocked me out. I lifted my ass and came down on him. "Fuck!" he cried out, smacking my ass. When I made circles, D'Mario met my thrusts with stronger ones and held me in position as he brought me down on him harder and faster. "Shit! I'm about to—Ohh!"

I hopped off after catching my breath and collapsed next to him on the bed. He'd earned a few minutes afterward. We laid in the bed with my back to him. D'Mario's breath on my neck made me want to get up, but I fought it. Then he rested his hand on my naked hip. I didn't want him to get too comfortable. After he dozed off, I snuck out of bed, grabbed my clothes, and got cleaned up in the bathroom.

The plan was to leave undetected, but as soon as I opened the door, D'Mario faced me on the bed. He already had on his sweats.

"It's the middle of the night. Why you gotta bounce right after every time?"

This routine quickly got annoying. We'd had a good time. That should have been enough. "Didn't I stay a bit?"

"Man, we finished like twenty minutes ago." He stood up but stayed near the bed.

"That's twenty minutes longer than I wanted to be here." I picked up my purse from the chair on the other side of the room. I needed to nip this in the bud. Staying with him wasn't happening and he kept fighting that fact.

"So, it's really like that? Who are you? Why are you so—"

"Please don't. I'm tired and I want to sleep in my bed."

"We can meet at your place next time. That way you won't have to leave like this."

"Not a good idea at all. Home space was never part of the deal. Never will be."

Why was he so damn needy? Men like him needed to be on a real dating site because his ass wanted someone to cuddle with. I wasn't the one.

"Eve, I'm not going to hurt you." The way he looked at me didn't change my mind. I had my reasons and didn't want to keep doing this to him.

"I didn't say you would."

"Then why can't you chill? Lay here. Let's talk about something."

"What do you think this is? 'Cause my idea was more

along a fuck and go type thing. I'm not tryna be with you, D'Mario."

"Damn, Eve. Who hurt you? Why you so closed up?"

"Because I didn't come here for this. You want too much."

"I only asked you to stay the whole night."

"And I said no more than once. I don't know you and I don't want to." That sounded worse out loud than it did in my head.

What was I arguing with this man for? This was exactly what I deserved. I swore to myself I'd stay off that damn app the last time. D'Mario definitely gave me the motivation I lacked to find men the traditional way at a bar or a club.

"Look, I'm sorry you don't like my ways. We don't have to do this again."

"Wait! That's not what I—"

"I need to go, okay. It's been good. Have a nice life."

I walked out of there like I'd dumped someone. Brother had some serious attachment issues. Or maybe I did. It didn't matter. We were done with the fun. Damn, it was good, though.

When I made it home, I took a shower to scrub him off of me and, hopefully, any weakness I'd almost developed from his damn tongue. I ran a bubble bath, lit some candles, and put on my Tank, Tyrese, and Ginuwine playlist. My last bottle of wine was halfway done, so I skipped the glass and brought the bottle in the tub. I soaked in hot water to remove the guilt of the night. D'Mario was only a tiny part of my guilt. He wasn't the first one I'd left behind, knowing they wanted more than I wanted to give.

To my surprise, most men I'd come across wanted more than just sex. Obviously, I kept choosing the wrong ones. They all made me seem like a fucked up person for not wanting more than what was between their legs. What they offered was medicine for me, not a cure. I didn't want the person attached to the appendage that kept me in this cycle. I was on that August Alsina "No Love" level. None for me.

I rested my head on my tub pillow and closed my eyes. I rubbed my hand from my breast across my belly, then reaching my bean as "On My Way" by Ginuwine played. The visuals from the best I'd ever had over the years ran across my mind as I strummed my bean like a guitar. The last image jolted me out of the zone.

*What the hell?* I couldn't even finish for fear of seeing him again. I didn't want him. Why would my reel even include Zak's dumb ass? I saw him but never had him and never would. What a way to ruin a good time.

# NINE

# Gianna

I'D SKIPPED CHURCH ON THE SAME SUNDAY FOR THE last ten years. After my life changed forever the day she left me, Mother's Day had turned into a mournful holiday. Churches perfected praising the mothers with a program put on by the youth and little gifts passed out to the mothers in the congregation.

I used to eagerly await Mother's Day as a kid because our church had us choose a poem to recite or write one of our own. As I got older, the more elaborate my gifts and ideas became. Home-cooked breakfasts and dinners, personal coupon books, her favorite Turtles candy, mother/daughter dates. You name it; I did it.

Well, I did things within my means. I'd save my lunch money and the cash from Mimi to buy something special. Putting a smile on Momma's face always brought me joy. She deserved all of it and more.

My mother was the best a girl could ask for. She was my friend in a way that made me comfortable to talk to her about anything. She'd listen to my long dreams or stories. If anything happened at school, I told her about it. Whenever something involved a student coming at me crazy, she assured me I had the right to knock their ass out if they put their hands on me. Not before. She taught me how to be emotionally tough, so no one could get to me with words. I still followed those teachings today.

Momma taught me to be self-sufficient and to never wholly depend on anyone but God. People always found new ways to disappoint and drop the ball, but God never did. I knew when I got older that her training came from her experiences with Blair. He was a no-show during my younger days. They were never together, but I guessed they were long enough for me to be here.

She never spoke kindly of him, so the fact that I'd allowed him in confused me. Momma hated the man. A woman with so much love in her heart had room to hate someone. I hadn't seen her lose her temper past some yelling or if she had to beat my ass for something stupid I'd said or did.

There weren't any men around when I was growing up. That part I did not understand. She was my mother, but she was a woman first. Not getting any regularly would've taken me out. Maybe having me distracted her from that need, but I highly doubted it.

Mother's Day hurt in a million different ways. I couldn't see her, hug her, hear her voice, or that loud ass laugh. With me, she seemed like the goofiest person on the planet, but no one outside our house saw that side of her. Those were my special memories. Seeing Momma dress up and lip-sync Anita Baker, Toni Braxton, Yolanda Adams, and even MC Lyte. She was strictly R&B, old hip-hop, and gospel. Nothing else made it to my ears until I was on my own.

My favorite times were us cuddling up watching reruns

of her favorite shows like *A Different World, In Living Color, Martin*, and the *Jamie Foxx Show*. Then there were *Girlfriends* and *The Game*. She never missed one, and neither did I once she let me watch them. If I wasn't with Janelle, you could find me cooking, playing cards, or watching something under my mom. Nothing ever lured me away from spending time with her like the other kids out and about.

Momma was a best friend who could beat my ass if I got out of line. I knew the boundaries and loved the closeness that created a bond still unbreakable today. Her word was Bible. What she said went with no questions asked. I respected her to know whatever she told me was for a reason and for my benefit.

I stretched my body across the couch, going through the photo album I made of the two of us. I was infamous for snapping away with my camera. This book housed a lot of random photos, but none from when I was a baby. They must've been in the storage unit. Momma and Mimi passed the photo fever down to me because they could fill a building with all the pictures they took and printed. I made a note on my phone to stop at the unit and search for them.

Blair texted me even though he knew Mother's Day was a no-contact day. I didn't want to waste it on any of the nonsense I dealt with daily. All of it qualified as nonsense because my life made no sense without her in it.

**Blair: I know today is hard on you. I just want you to know that I'm thinking about you. We love and miss you. Don't let today make you sad. Celebrate what an amazing mother you had. She lives on in you.**

That half-bottle of Fireball wanted to come out on him.

What the hell would he know? He didn't know her or what type of mother she was. I had to be respectful, right?

Nah.

**Me: What do you know? You dropped us like we were nothing. Don't act like you understand my pain.**

I tossed my phone to the other sofa. It landed on the floor and stayed there, so I'd have no reason to read his response if he'd respond. Blair and the truth didn't get along. Whenever I spoke it, he denied it.

My phone dinged. Today was not the day to piss me off. The phone would stay where it was, away from me. Then I convinced myself that Janelle may be the one who texted. She knew I didn't want to talk, but sometimes she'd send a text about my mother to let me know she cared.

I weakly rose to my feet. Sipping on cinnamon whiskey after having only eaten a bowl of cereal wasn't my most brilliant move. I'd only drank three glasses with ice. The ice counted as dilution when it melted, so it couldn't be that bad. My eyes itched and felt heavy, but I made it to my phone to see who'd texted.

**Blair: I understand that I have to talk to you about things but today is not the time. We'll talk later. I love you.**

Whatever. Blair wouldn't get to me with that. I was too hungry and dizzy to go back and forth, even though a good cussing out would make me feel better. I ordered Chinese. General Tso with egg rolls and fried shrimp as appetizers. Enough grease and salt to sober me up a bit.

Unhealthy food and season five of *A Different World*. Momma loved the last few episodes when Joe Morton, a.k.a. Byron, came into the picture. I felt like she watched it with me. All up to the wedding that never happened. She usually rooted for TV love but avoided the real thing. Another part of her I'd taken on.

———

I FOUND BLAIR SITTING AT A VACANT PAVILION AT THE park. He'd been asking me to meet with him for weeks. Even had his wife reach out to make this happen. I wasn't in the mood, but they were persistent.

He stood up as I approached him and had the nerve to open his arms for a hug. As much as it would have pleased me to pass on an embrace, I didn't hate the man. He got points for trying. We sat after he released me.

"Shana thought the time had come for me to tell you the whole truth about me and your mother."

"I learned it by heart. You left her after you knocked her up and didn't care for over twenty years. You blamed your ex-wife, saying she forbid you to see me. The truth remains the same today."

"Gia, it's imperative that you listen and be an adult about this."

I stood up to leave. Ain't no way that was going to fly this Saturday morning. He took hold of my wrist, trying to pull me back down. "Sit down. I have to say this."

"What is there to say, Blair? Your absence spoke volumes. You never showed your face. Those are facts."

"So the real reason doesn't matter?"

"Excuses usually don't. Either show up or don't. We don't have to guess which route you took."

"Gia, please understand that things were more complicated than what you were told. Out of love and respect for your mother, I allowed her truth to be your truth. I wish you'd stop treating me like I'm some evil person. We both made mistakes. Your mother and I did."

"Was I one of them? Is that what you're trying to tell me?"

"Absolutely not. You are the greatest thing that ever happened to me and my biggest regret in life was not being there to raise you side-by-side with Elaine."

I smacked my lips. "Sure it is."

Blair exhaled loud enough for me to turn his way. I assumed he was trying to keep from getting upset with me.

"Did she tell you I wanted to marry her?"

I snickered, knowing that shit was a lie.

"Gia, I not only loved your mother, but I was so far gone *in* love with her. Before I went away to medical school, I asked her to come with me. Your grandmother forbade it."

"You never loved her. Y'all only messed around a few times, made me, and then you bounced and got married soon after that. Momma said you must've been cheating on your first wife with her."

Blair leaned back to release a deep belly laugh. "What?" He dragged his hand over his face. "I assumed she didn't want you to learn of the actual story, but I had no idea she completely made one up."

"What are you saying? My momma lied to me?"

"She told you what she thought best at the time. I won't call her a liar. Truth bender?" He chuckled and shook his head.

"That's not funny, and I don't believe you. Why the hell would she make anything up?"

"I don't have the answer for that. They kept me away. Your grandmother didn't want me to take your mother from Houston. Elaine said her mom didn't want to be alone. I had to leave her behind. Shortly after, she told me you were on the way. That's when I proposed. If we got married, Eleanora would possibly let her go with me."

"You're telling me y'all fell in love, you proposed, and she turned it down? Make that make sense to me. If it's the truth, why would she not accept?"

"Gia, I really wish she was here to answer that. I concluded she didn't want to leave Eleanora by herself. I promised we'd move back because I planned to work in the medical center here. It still wasn't enough."

Mimi didn't seem like the type that would hold her daughter back for her own sake. My grandmother sacrificed a lot and supported my mom. Her stopping Momma from a happy ending made no sense.

"My momma would never lie to me. Especially about you. Why did she hate you if you're such a great guy? You weren't there. Why would she say you didn't want anything to do with me? Come on now." I stood up, ready to go because I no longer believed he took me seriously with this bogus ass story.

"Probably because my ex-wife didn't allow me to see you because she knew the truth."

"What truth?"

"That I was in love with Elaine. We got married because her father wanted me as a son-in-law. He had a practice here that I wanted to work at after I finished school and my residency. Love had nothing to do with that arrangement."

"You're going all out, huh? I will applaud you for having thought of everything in this elaborate story. Because that's all it is. Fiction."

I turned to walk away, then looked back at him. "My mother was strong, gorgeous, smart, brave, broken, and honest about it. You broke her perception of men and she warned me to be aware of those like you. Liars and leavers, as she put it. I'm done for the day. Thank you for trying, I guess."

Blair appeared defeated by the time I finally walked away. I wasn't about to sit and listen to him speak lies about my momma. Not today. Or ever. Not a dime he threw at me would change that.

# TEN

# Gianna

Janelle wanted to go out. No one really needed a reason to hang, but clubbing with her brother and her man didn't appeal to me. She'd be all over Cameron while I'd have to entertain myself, since I had no one to dance with. It took a lot to get me on the dance floor by myself.

With a group of my girls, hell yes. Being the third wheel dry humping and grinding on the air? Nah. As soon as we walked through the entrance, all eyes were on us. Then I realized those eyes were actually on Zakari. He wasn't that damn fine. Well, maybe, but still.

The single women watched him like he was a piece of meat they all wanted to devour. As soon as it became clear to a blind man that we weren't together, they jumped on him. I mean, those women came up asking him to dance or to get him a drink. Others flat out offered the goods.

While Zak had his hands full, Janelle and Cameron tried pulling me from our section to dance. No way I'd dance with her and her man. I encouraged them to have fun as a couple and not worry about me. Janelle refused to leave me at first, so I pulled my phone out to act like she bored me enough to play games. That always ticked her off enough to walk away. It did the job.

Shot number three had me feeling all kinds of sexy, joining them on the dance floor. My slight movements made me forget I was in a public place. With no man to grind on, I pushed my ass against nothing at all and didn't trip about it. When Sammie's "Times 10" purred through the speakers, I zoned out.

All the swaying and rubbing on my body was better than having some no-good, nothing-ass dude on me.

"You really letting loose, huh?" Janelle got in my face, dancing along with me.

"Girl!" I dropped it real slow for the hell of it. "I needed this so bad."

"You look good doing it, too. Niggas breaking their necks to get a glimpse."

My head fell back, releasing a belly laugh. "I ain't worried about no man tonight. It's all about me enjoying myself."

"Uh-huh. You feeling yourself so much that Zak is over there gawking."

"What?!" I slowly twirled around and caught him staring at my ass.

Janelle guffawed. "Looks like little brother never got over his crush."

"Crush?" My head tilted.

"Girl, please. He been crushing on you from day one."

"Hell, naw! That little fucker was mean and annoying as hell. Still is!"

I grabbed my girl to switch positions, so he'd stop looking at me. It worked. Zak's attention returned to the big booty girl giving him the business on this dance floor.

"Yeah, well, it looks like he still wants you."

"Eww! Why are you even telling me this? He's your little brother. That's off limits."

"Ay! Ay! Ay!" Janelle got distracted and pushed her ass on her own man, who just returned from the restroom.

Zak? Not an option. I would admit that he'd somehow gotten sexy as hell. Linebacker body, beard game strong, lips made for biting, and... And what the hell was I talking about? Hell, no. It was time to get a drink and sit my ass down. No more shots. Things hadn't gotten *that* bad. I wasn't about to be looking at his ass that way.

At the bar, I waited for the female bartender to prepare my drink. Someone rubbed my lower back. I smiled, thinking it was Zak, and found myself disappointed at D'Mario's smirk.

"I thought that was you, Eve." He leaned on the bar. "Damn, you look good."

"Thank you, but I don't know you." The bartender handed me my mojito. Before I handed her the card to pay, D'Mario placed his hand on mine. "Nah, put it on my tab." He winked at her while giving her his card.

"I really appreciate it. Now, I need to go. My people are over there waiting on me, so..."

He pressed his lips together. "Oh, I get it. I'm good enough to fuck but not to chill with."

"It's not even like that. We did this dance already. We're done messing around. You don't respect my rules. We don't want the same thing. I'm not looking for a relationship."

"Since when did dancing become a relationship? We're both here. Why can't we—"

I smacked my lips. "You're right. I'm being extra." *It wasn't that serious.* "Come on."

He followed me to our reserved section. One thing I wouldn't do was put my drink down and walk away.

Sipping while he kept me company would do. D'Mario told me who he came with, and I did the same, pointing them out on the dance floor. As soon as I finished my drink, we joined my friends instead of his.

Janelle's eyes widened at the temporary addition to our group. I shook my head to make sure she understood it was nothing. She shrugged and kept on grooving.

One thing I couldn't deny was that D'Mario's sex appeal oozed from every part of him. Not wanting anything past sex didn't stem from anything personal. He knew how to touch me with clothes on.

The man kind of made me a little happy we ran into each other. Winding my hips and grinding against him was better than doing it on a total stranger, since his erection didn't freak me out as much. I'd seen and touched it. It didn't belong to me, but it brought some comfort.

When I turned to wrap my arms around D'Mario's neck, Zak's eyes were glued to mine. His raised brow confused me.

Five songs later, my feet begged for a break. I tugged on Janelle and nodded toward our section. On the way, she said something to Zak, and we headed to my feet's salvation. D'Mario sat next to me, with Janelle on my other side.

Cameron had my girl's full attention as she giggled. I sensed D'Mario's eyes on me as if we'd behave the same. His presence now made me squirm because he was part of a life no one else was privy to. His fine ass needed to go.

"So, hey, we're leaving soon. Maybe we can hook up later this week or something."

He inched closer, kissing my neck. "Why not tonight?"

"Because I'm with my people. That'll be awkward."

D'Mario looked at me sideways. "Eve, it's not like we

hadn't gone there. The way you lookin' right now…" He bit that damn bottom lip.

"Tempting, but I need to go home. They are my ride." I gestured toward Janelle and Cameron.

"Baby, I can be your ride. Let me take you home. I can put you to bed the way you need it." *What was with all the baby stuff in public?* I didn't care how he made my body want to jump on him, calling me baby when it wasn't even like that was a turnoff.

"It's not a good night."

Zak came to the section with his newfound groupie. He checked his phone before looking at his sister. "Ay, y'all want anything else before I close the tab?"

"We good, but thanks," Cameron told him after briefly breaking away from the intense energy between him and Janelle.

Zak tapped my knee. "Gia, you good?" I faintly nodded.

"Gia? I thought your name was Eve." D'Mario stated loudly, trying to talk over the music. Only the music transitioned right before he opened his mouth, making it sound like he was yelling. Shit, he might as well had once all eyes were on me.

I locked eyes with Janelle, who'd come up for air, and I shook my head for her to say nothing. "It is! He just calls me that as an inside joke."

Zak sucked his teeth and left for the bar with the chick that had latched onto him an hour ago. She even gave me a little side-eye with lashes too big for her face. She'd take flight if she fluttered her eyes too much.

"Who is he?" D'Mario stood as if he had any reason to be mad.

I stepped away from our section. I didn't want anyone to hear him or to inquire about him. A fool could see that this wasn't the first time we'd met. "Zak's a family friend. Chill out. Matter of fact, bye. Thank you for your time tonight. I had fun. Goodnight."

D'Mario's head jerked back, looking offended. I didn't owe him a damn thing. The quicker he understood that fact the better. "That's how you do it?" His stance was firm in front of me, hands clasped together near his groin.

I crossed my arms to show him he'd met his match if he wanted to be stupid. "D'Mario, that's how you're making it. We ain't together. You sounding all...bothered. I don't care why at this point." Janelle and Cameron were waiting for me. Once I had no real excuse to keep them waiting, my eyes fell back on D'Mario's. "Anyway, I'm out. Bye."

D'Mario's head dropped to the side with his lips pressed together. After nodding, he waved me off and disappeared. "What the hell was that? You giving out different names now?" Janelle laughed in my face.

"That ain't nothing. Y'all ready?" I held her by the waist since she'd put her arm around my neck. Cameron led the way toward the exit once we met back up with Zak.

My ass could barely walk straight and these damn shoes were about to have me on the floor. "Hold on. I'll be out there in a second." I stopped at the bar for a bottle of water and to switch my shoes. I had some thin slippers in my clutch. A lesson my college years had taught me. Usually, there was no need for them because drinking too much in public wasn't my norm. Tonight had gotten away from me, but not so much to forget these.

I headed toward the exit with my shoes in one hand and the water bottle in the other. The humidity hit me all in the face, but I was happy to go home and sleep this buzz off. Before I made it to everybody, D'Mario grabbed my arm. I tried pulling away, but his grip tightened.

"D'Mario, what the hell? Let go."

He raised his hands in surrender. I straightened myself up. "What is it?" This proved exactly why I didn't date. Men tended to be so possessive after a little taste.

"That was real fucked up in there, but I'll forgive you if you make it up to me." He wrapped his arm around me and pulled me into him.

I tried to wriggle from his grasp. "I told you no. Not tonight or ever again. You doing too much." He laughed at my failed attempt to get away from him. "Boy, let me the fuck go!"

Out of nowhere, Zak pushed D'Mario back while grabbing hold of me at the same time. "You okay?"

"Yeah," I answered, picking up the shoe that dropped. When my ass brushed up against Zak, he didn't move. A confusing tingle shot through my love pocket. *Not now, Gia.* I had to remember who Zak was.

"Nigga, what the fuck? She yo' bitch or something?" D'Mario ran up to get in Zak's face, but I stood between them. My back was against Zak while I reached out to keep D'Mario at bay.

"She ain't nobody's bitch. Watch yo' fuckin' mouth!" Zak held me, pretending like I had the power to stop him from getting to D'Mario if he really wanted to. That man's arm wrapped around me almost made me forget the problem.

My attention shifted from my confusingly wet panties to the man before us. D'Mario's chest rose and fell, causing my heart to speed race. I didn't want any kind of shit going down on my behalf. "Please, just stop," I yelled.

"Eve, you said you didn't have a man." D'Mario's regard was now on me, face twitching. His anger was extreme for what we'd done only a few times.

"I don't."

"Why he keep calling you that?" Zak asked, still holding me close.

"Look, let's forget anything happened and get on with our night, okay? We'll go this way and you go that way. Everything is all good." I stepped back after my last word, but Zak's big ass barely moved.

Zak brought his head closer to my ear. "You know this nigga?"

D'Mario snorted. "If she says she don't, her pussy does."

"Whoa! Don't be putting my business out like that," I told him.

Zak chuckled. "But she gave you a fake name. You in yo' feelings?"

I checked around for help, but no one else was there. *Where was the damn bouncer? Shouldn't someone be outside?* Janelle and Cameron must've left. The girl with Zak had gone, too.

"Okay, boys. Are you done?" I turned around and pushed Zak to walk in the opposite direction toward the parking lot before facing D'Mario. "This...whatever it was is forever done."

Zak hadn't walked away. He'd only taken a few steps when I pushed him.

D'Mario sucked his teeth loud as hell. We were only about ten feet from each other. "You'll be back. The way I have your ass screaming and shit. You'll be back on my dick in no time."

"Fuck you. Better yet, I'm never fucking you again. Trust. Your shit ain't all that."

All I heard was "bitch" as we walked away. Zak stopped to engage with D'Mario's ignorant ass. I interlocked our fingers so he'd stay focused. Zak damn near pulled me along the way once his feet started moving. His long legs had me power walking to keep up. I didn't really have a choice, since he still had my hand in his.

"Where's Janelle?" I finally got out. Zak dragged me behind him like he was mad. It shouldn't've gone down like that.

"She left with Cam. They asked me to drop you off."

"I wish someone would've told me the damn plan."

"Guess you were too busy with yo' man." He kept on walking.

I smacked my lips. "Don't do that shit with me, Zakari. He ain't my man and that's none of your business, anyway."

"Ain't nobody said it was, Gia."

Zak opened the passenger door for me. "Where's your girl?" I asked while getting in.

He scoffed. "That's none of your business." He walked to the other side to get in.

The man sat there in the driver's seat. His breaths were slow and heavy, but no words. I didn't want to talk about D'Mario and hoped he didn't either. I waited out the silence for at least three minutes, watching him clench his jaw repeatedly from the side.

"Um, why are we not leaving?"

Zak's ass needed to get with it and pull off. His head pivoted my way, making stern eye contact. "That's the niggas you fuck with now?"

Not that it was any of his damn business. "Not really. Can we go? Take me to my car, please."

"You can barely walk straight. You're going home."

I put on my seatbelt. "Whatever. Can we go then?" No reason to contest. I was in no condition to drive, but his attitude made me want to risk it for a second.

"Gia, you are so much better than that shit. Why you even—"

"Zak, I already know this. It was something that happened a few times. I didn't think I'd ever see his ass out anywhere. This really isn't important. If you're taking me home, take me." I rolled my eyes at his judgmental ass. He could take a female home on the first night, but had the nerve to look at me crazy for being a grown-ass woman.

He finally turned on the damn car after staring at me for what felt like forever. That shit felt cold.

We rode the whole way listening to music. I was relieved that he'd left it alone. I told him to drop me off at the front of my building, but he refused. He'd claimed he wanted to make sure I got inside my place safely and insisted on walking me in. We'd see about that.

# ELEVEN

# Zakari

SHIT DIDN'T SIT WELL WITH ME ABOUT GIA MESSING with low ass niggas. I had too much respect for her to let that go. Yes, I gave her a hard time with jokes, but that's what we did. Always been that way.

She stared out the window the entire drive to her place. I ain't have nothing else to say to her at first. I was... disappointed.

*What was she doing?* Gia could have any man she wanted. Picking randos was so beneath her.

Seeing that dude grab on her had me heated. Then realizing he'd for real had her, touched her. It was bad enough watching her dance on him, but knowing they'd done more had me tripping.

If anyone came at Janelle crazy, I'd go for the dome. Same with Gia. Stupid crush aside.

When we pulled up to the building, her crazy ass thought I'd let her walk alone in the middle of the night. I didn't care how much she was in her feelings about me calling her out. I'd make sure she got in safely.

Gia opened the garage door. The last time I parked on

the street and came in through the lobby. All these damn turns up to the sixth floor irritated me, but the closer we got to her floor, I had to say something.

I parked, ready to apologize if I came off hard, but she hopped out before I turned off the car. "Gia?" I yelled after she slammed my door. She didn't stop for even a second. I turned the car off and went after her. "Gia, wait!" A three-second jog caught me up. "Damn, can you wait up? What's up with you?"

Gia turned around with her arms swinging near her hips. "Look little boy, I don't need no damn babysitter. Nor do I need yo' ass judging me about what I do with my—" She stopped herself and took a deep breath. "Get in your car and leave. I'm safe. Thank you for the ride."

"No. I'll leave when you're inside. I don't wanna hear shit else about it."

Gia's darkened eyes set on mine like I'd challenged her and she'd accepted. "Who the fuck you think you talking to? I'm not one of your little hoes. I'm a grown ass woman and I do not need your help."

"A grown ass woman who gives out a fake name, huh?" I dropped my head and laughed. "Yeah, real ladylike. I should've let old dude finish whatever he was doing at the club. Miss Grown Ass can handle herself when a nigga grabs her drunk ass."

"I'm not drunk. I'm tipsy. There's a difference. Stop acting like he was trying to kidnap me."

"Shit, who knows? He could've if I wasn't there. 'Cause that's the shit that happens when you go around fucking people you don't know."

Gia stepped back, balling her fist like it was about to go down. "You little motherfucker. You know nothing about me. How dare you stand there and look down on me? You ain't no better. You were leaving with a girl you just met. Did you give her the same speech? She didn't know yo' stupid ass no more than I knew him."

She had a point, but this wasn't about me. "Whatever, G. Let's get you inside so I can go."

Gia spun around and marched to the door of her hallway. She used her fob to open it. We walked all the way down the hall to get to her place. As soon as I saw the door, I had to use the restroom.

"We're here. You can go now. Handle your duties for the night with your females besties that you respect completely. That's what is, right? Not random bitches, but best friends."

I smacked my lips. She always had shit to say. "I need to use the restroom."

"Hmph. Sounds like a you problem. I'm sure one of your many girls has a bathroom. Bye." Gia unlocked and opened the door before quickly stepping inside. She turned to close it in my face, but I stuck my foot in the way first.

"Man, quit playing. Just let me use your bathroom and I'll leave."

When she didn't move, I pushed the door with a little more force. "I didn't say you can come into my house, Zakari. Go pee outside. I'm sure my place isn't good enough for self-righteous assholes like yourself."

"Ay, watch yo' mouth." I closed the door behind me. She sucked her teeth and rolled her eyes for the millionth time. Them suckers should be turned inside out by now. No matter what she did, no matter how disrespectful, I wanted her. I wanted to strip her down and make love to her on the island she leaned on once she moved out of the way. That attitude didn't help any of it die down.

The curls in her hair rested in a high ponytail that I

wanted to grab while kissing her hard. Her ass was there, but it didn't take over her body. It was more than enough to hold onto or smack from behind. I bit my bottom lip at the thought.

"What the hell are you staring at? Go to the bathroom since you so rudely barged in here to do it."

That urge decreased as another took over. I walked up to her and she stood firm on her bare feet in the kitchen. "Nigga, don't be running up on me like you gon' do someth—"

My mouth covered hers long enough until her initial attempt to fight me passed. Her palms pressed against my chest, but with less force. Gia threw her arms around my neck, accepting the intrusion of my tongue. She sucked on it long enough to have me rock hard and ready to put a baby in her stomach right then.

She moaned into my mouth and I damn near lost it. "Wait! No! We can't do this," she spoke onto my lips.

"Why?" I asked between pecks. "That kiss said something different."

"You started it. Zak, you're like a little brother to me." She stepped backward.

It was my turn for the eyerolling. "Man, stop with all that 'little' shit. Ain't nothing about me little. Believe that shit. I ain't in no way related to you." I pulled her back into me, pressing up against her nipples poking through her top.

Gia dropped her head and laughed. "First of all, you just basically called me a hoe outside. Second, we're not doing this."

I let her go. "So, you can do this with random niggas but I can't get a chance."

"I don't do *this*. I don't kiss them. Stop calling them

random. I could've had a full-blown relationship with that man. How would you know the difference?"

"Based on what you told me in the car, you didn't. From your defensiveness, he ain't the first one."

"Stop acting like you know me. You don't." That must've pushed a button since she walked past me and into the living room.

I followed her but stood next to the couch instead of falling onto it like she did. "I know enough, Gia. If you do it only for the sex, I can handle that for you."

Her belly laughs made it clear she didn't believe me. My ego could deal with it since I hadn't touched her yet.

"I am not about to be another one in your current rotation, Zakari. I do what I do because I don't want a relationship."

"So, you'd rather meet up with strangers who could hurt you? That's better than being with someone who would do anything to protect you?"

"Anything? We ain't even cool like that. Besides, I'm a frog prince, remember?"

I laughed at the way she said it. "Now you know I be playing with you. You are nothing less than perfection." My eyes slowly ran from her feet to her lips, then her cute nose, and those dark browns she stared at me from. "You are more beautiful than the last time you were here. I haven't stopped thinking about you since."

"Zak, don't play with me. I may be a little under the influence, but I ain't stupid."

"I'm not, G. For real. Besides, I kissed you. So, you're no longer a frog." I got a pillow thrown at me for that one. She aimed for my face, but my elbow blocked it. "For real though. If you only want sex, why can't I do that for you?"

"Because you're you. Plus, Janelle would lose it."

"She ain't gotta know. No one does. It'll be our little secret and I'll know that you ain't putting yourself in danger fucking strange men."

"Strange? Really? D'Mario wasn't strange. He just couldn't handle what I put on him. I don't want to do the same to you. Your soft ass will probably try to marry me."

"You funny. I was thinking the same thing. See, you'd be the one begging me to remove everyone else from my rotation, as you say, and want to keep me all to yourself."

"I don't do relationships, Zak."

"I didn't ask you for one. Let me take care of you. Your body, at least. If you change your mind about being with someone else, we'll stop."

"So, wait! I can't be with someone else, but you can?"

"Hey, you're the one who don't do relationships. If I cut them off, then that will go against your policy."

"Oh, you tryna be funny."

"I'm not. I'm only tryna do some thangs to you. And protect you, of course."

"What if I need protection from you?"

"I can do that too. I keep protection with me at all times."

She chucked a rubber coaster at me and missed. "You know what I'm talking about, crazy. I don't do relationships because I don't want to get hurt."

"Then you have nothing to worry about. I won't hurt you."

Gia took in a long breath. "Things will be weird between us."

I sat next to her, looking at her from the side. "That ship sailed. I tasted your tongue. Felt your lips. No matter what happens, those are now ingrained in my brain."

"Already catching feelings."

I caught those years ago. The reality of them being anything more than in my head was something different. "So, we doing this or what?" I asked with a smile that I hoped helped my case.

"Come here."

I leaned closer to her. Gia stared up at me. Her eyes moved back and forth to each of mine until an unsure smile spread across her face. She placed a palm on both of my cheeks. I let her have all control so my eagerness wouldn't ruin it. Once she closed her eyes, I braced for her lips. Holding my breath in disbelief. Yeah, I'd kissed her minutes ago, but this meant her acceptance. She'd let me in.

Gia's lips pressed against mine. My dick throbbed so hard it hurt. I couldn't and wouldn't stop my tongue from invading her mouth once again. Only this time, she invited it. Her tongue swiped across mine, and I repeated the motion, tasting liquor and heat.

She pulled away. "What are we doing?"

"Whatever you want."

One more kiss and she jumped from the couch. "Zak, no. I can't do this tonight. Maybe I had too much to drink. Then you come in here looking like *that*. I'm not in my right mind and neither are you."

I dropped my head and closed my eyes for a few seconds. So close to everything I'd always wanted. I needed her to want it, too. "A'ight." Standing to my feet, I adjusted my jeans and boxers.

Her eyes widened. "Wait, that was your..."

I followed her gaze to my groin, then laughed. Gia's mouth was open. "My what? Say it."

She didn't. Instead, she walked over to me, squinting. "Let me see it."

"Nah, that's for willing participants only. You'll see it when you want it."

"Zakari, stop being a baby. I wanna see." Gia grabbed my dick through my jeans. I tried to dodge her, but her hand brushed up against it. She gasped. "Damn! Do I need to change my mind?"

"Nope. Like you said, you need to be sober." I did my best not to smirk at her discovery.

She smacked her lips. "Oh, now you wanna listen to me."

When she poked her lips to the side, my dick twitched. I saw them on me in a flash. Damn, she had sexy lips. It seemed like my first time really seeing them now that I knew how they felt.

"We'll talk. I gotta go."

"I thought you had to use the bathroom."

"I do. You keep distracting me."

"Me? Boy please. You're the one tryna get it."

"You made it clear you ain't giving it more than once."

"Yeah, yeah. Go use it so I can go to sleep."

I did as she told me and relieved myself in her bathroom. On my way out, she gave me this look like she'd considered my offer. Gia didn't give me the typical "you get on my nerves" face. This one had a "you could get it" vibe I wished I could cash in tonight. Instead, I walked out the door after she teased me with a peck on the cheek.

No way should it have been that hard to walk out. Usually, when I went to a woman's house, she'd invited me over to do exactly what I wanted to do to Gia. Tonight, that shit tested my patience. If one chick wasn't available, another one was on standby. Gia had my ass willing to wait on her. The way those hungry eyes followed me; it wouldn't be too much longer.

## TWELVE

# Gianna

On the way to Janelle's for a game night with her and Cameron's friends, she told me she had a surprise for me. I had one for her, too, if I ever conjured up enough guts to say anything.

Her damn brother had given me blue bean on multiple occasions since the club a few weeks ago. The week after that night, they'd both invited me to yet another club. I'd declined.

Avoiding Zakari had become a requirement for my sanity, or at least for the cover-up of my temporary insanity. All I saw was his dumb, sexy ass I-can't-go-there face.

He could kiss. Like really kiss. The kind that lingered on after the fact.

When I got there, Janelle introduced me to two couples. The women were her friends. I hadn't met them sooner because I hadn't wanted to. She'd tried to get me to go out with them a few times. My ass was weird with meeting new people. Especially friends of friends. With my absence, they'd probably thought they knew her better than I did. That shit annoyed the hell out of me.

Cameron was acting funny, asking me personal dating questions. Janelle shrugged it off. For her, I kept it sweet and simply told him what I'd told everyone else. I wasn't down for what they had. I loved being single and unattached.

Once he let me off the hook, I grabbed a beer from the fridge. I should've passed on this night. Being under a blanket snuggled with any of the hundred books I hadn't read appealed to me more than being around these people. Plus, everyone was boo'd up. There had to be a way to get out of this.

"What's up, Zak?" One of Janelle's friends greeted him. I was so busy coming up with ways to get back home, I didn't realize he'd come. Hell, I hoped they did not invite him. Janelle never told me she hung out with him this damn much.

Still being antisocial in the kitchen, I kept my back facing everyone. He probably wouldn't notice me. Zak's voice made the entrance to my lake throb like she'd missed him. She didn't know him like that and never would.

Someone walked up on me. *Please be Janelle. Please be Janelle.*

"Why you over here by yourself?" *Dammit, Zakari!*

*Play it cool, Gia.* "I'm getting a drink."

He flashed a smile with his chuckle. "G, I've been here a few minutes and you ain't moved from this spot. You need help with that?" He pointed to my unopened bottle.

"Uh, no. I got it."

We stood there staring at each other like no one else was there. I broke away first. *Why did he have to look at me like that?* My natural dam had failed me and my panties caught a little something.

I wanted to bite his lip, suck his tongue, among other

things. That damn facial hair neatly trimmed into a healthy beard teased me. Facial hair gave a manly vibe. One that his ass used against me. Even if not on purpose. I wanted to run my fingers through it.

"What y'all talking about?" Janelle snuck up on us.

"Nothing, just getting a beer," I spat out. The damn thing wasn't even cold anymore.

"She been holding on that bottle looking all dazed. Somebody got yo' girl shook."

Janelle's jaw dropped. "Really? Why you didn't tell me? Who is it?"

"Nobody. Your idiot brother is talking out the side of his neck like always."

"Sure about that?" He raised a brow.

I stared at him, wanting to slap him, but any physical interaction was a no-go. "Are you sure you don't wanna get out of my face?"

"Y'all are always at it. But, um, where's your date?" Janelle asked her brother.

"Date?" I asked with too much concern in my voice. Both of them looked at me. Her with surprise, him with a smirk.

"No, I mean, we're supposed to bring dates?" I cleared my throat. "You didn't tell me this was a couples thing. I can go home then."

"Not so fast. Cameron's friend is on his way."

"So?" I didn't get what that meant.

Zak answered for her. "So no odd numbers."

Janelle bit the corner of her mouth with both brows hiked. "Well yes, but Cam thinks you might like him."

"What?" Zak and I blurted.

Janelle laughed at us. "Okay twins. Why do you even care?" she asked Zak.

"Because I didn't bring anyone."

She placed her hand on his shoulder. "Oh, yeah. Your female friends are only women of the night."

He shrugged her hand off. "Ay, they ain't prostitutes. Just friends."

"That you screw," I added.

"You would know." He looked me up and down.

"Wait, what? What does that mean?" Janelle's eyes went between Zak's and mine. "Have y'all—"

I scrunched my face to lay it on heavy. "Hell, no! Come on now."

"You have been weird lately. Not showing up for Zak's party."

"That's because I don't like him."

"If you say so."

"So! I definitely say so."

Zak stayed quiet with a stupid expression, feeding her suspicion. She was wrong about what she'd suggested happened. So, technically, I didn't lie.

"Well, he's on his way. His name is Trevor. He's he is tall, dark, sexy, and successful." Nelle's grin was worse than the Cheshire Cat.

I folded my arms across my chest. "Good for him."

Zak got a beer from the fridge and left us in the kitchen. I assumed to avoid whatever his sister would say about this guy.

"Gia, I get that you are against the relationship thing, but promise me you will give him a try. He's a really great guy. You might like him."

"No promises."

"Well, at least be nice."

"Okay, okay. Damn! You don't leave stuff alone."

"I don't."

We joined the rest of the party after I switched out my beer for a colder one. I sat next to Zak only because I didn't want to sit with Trevor once he arrived.

Janelle had the food set up on the bar and announced for us to eat. I took her up on it and made me a plate. She made mainly finger foods. The heaviest item was chicken Alfredo and garlic bread. The same way Shana made it. Janelle had been getting some cooking lessons.

A knock at the door sped my heart up. Janelle opened the door to a man holding a bottle of 1800 tequila. Cameron got loud for a quiet guy. He was too happy to see this man. Trevor, however, was everything Janelle described and then some. Tall, dark, and sexy enough to pull out a "damn" when I got a good view.

Zak smacked his lips, since he was close enough to hear me. "He ain't all that. Shut up."

"You shut up. He could get it under other circumstances."

He turned to face me better. "Did you really just say that shit? After what we—"

"Gia, this is Trevor." Cameron caught us off guard with that damn Kofi Siriboe lookalike. The facial hair and everything.

"Hi, Trevor. Nice to meet you." I lifted my hand for a shake and he covered it with both hands.

"You as well, Gia. I've heard a lot about you, but no one mentioned how beautiful you are."

That corny line actually pulled a giggle from my lips. "Aww, thank you."

"You're welcome." His gaze sent a chill down my spine. It was like he was imagining what I looked like under these clothes. Okay, I was doing that and hoped those eyes of his wondered the same.

Meanwhile, Zakari stared straight ahead like the man wasn't standing in front of us.

"Oh, and this is Zak, Janelle's brother," Cameron added after what seemed like ten minutes of silence.

Zak gave him a nod, nothing more. The standing men narrowed their eyes at each other before moving on.

Cameron introduced Trevor to everyone else and we finally got into the games. Janelle made it known that her brother didn't have a date, so the numbers were off. With teams of two, mine had an unfair advantage. Trevor and Zakari were my two fine-ass teammates and what they did to my senses was complete torture. Belly fluttering with each knee tap or high five. Panties needing a replacement when they whispered anything in my ear. All G-rated stuff.

We'd started with Mad Gab, which gave me a chance to stare at Trevor's dark lips that contrasted his perfect white teeth. He couldn't keep a straight face whenever I had to read the nonsense on the cards. Zak didn't help us at all on that one. The boy sounded like he was illiterate. Granted, we weren't reading actual words.

Pictionary gave us the W, but no one acknowledged it with an extra member. Cards Against Humanity was every person for themselves. I'd suggested Janelle buy that one. My Miami girls and I played it more than anything else. Only two other people had played it before. No one wanted to stop. The first hour and a half felt like minutes. We took a break to chill and refill our drinks and plates.

I stayed seated with Trevor while Zak got up with everyone else. "You enjoying yourself?" Trevor asked, smiling like he knew he could have me.

"I am. More than I thought. Thanks to you."

"I'm glad to hear that." His shoulders relaxed.

"Cameron said you'd probably give me a hard time tonight. I'm happy he was wrong."

I rolled my eyes. "Janelle probably told him that since I don't really date much. Trust me, she gave me the 'be nice' speech tonight. It wasn't so hard to do. You're a cool guy."

Trevor placed his hand on his chest like he that touched him. We both laughed. "Well, since you think so. What would you say if I asked you out?"

"Hmm. I guess you'd have to ask."

He cleared his throat, straightened his posture, and fixed an invisible tie. "So, Gia, would you like to go out with me sometime?"

I scrunched my face before displaying a smile. "I'd like that, Trevor. Yeah."

"Here." Zak handed me a beer I never asked for, with a bit too much attitude in his throat.

"Uh, thank you?" I held it in my hand, watching him avoid eye contact.

Zak snorted. "Thought you might want another one."

"Okay." I shrugged and shook my head.

Trevor stood up. "I'm gonna grab something to eat."

He pulled another wide-ass smile out of me for no reason at all. "Okay."

"Do you want anything?" he asked, then narrowed his eyes at Mr. DoingTooMuch when Zak sucked his teeth loud as hell.

I touched his forearm to get his attention back to me. "I'm good. Thanks."

Zakari sat down when Trevor walked away. "Why you being funky?"

"What? What I do?" he asked with a lost look.

"Here," I mimicked him from earlier. "What's all that?"

"If you don't want the damn beer I'll drink it."

I waved him off. "Whatever, Zakari."

"Yeah, whatever with you and your little date."

I chuckled. "Really? Is that why you got an attitude?"

"I ain't got nothing."

"You damn right you don't."

He smacked his lips. "You can stop talking."

"You don't tell me what to do with yo' childish ass. 'You can stop talking.'" I mocked him in a baby's voice.

"What the hell is wrong with y'all?" Janelle stood in front of us. We weren't whispering, but I didn't think we were loud enough for anyone to know what we were saying. "Y'all always fighting. If I didn't know better, I'd think y'all were together."

I quickly shook my head. "How you come up with that if we're fighting?"

"Because I know both of y'all crazy behinds. This level of tension ain't normal unless y'all saw each other naked."

A gasp came from behind us. When I turned around, Cameron stood behind the couch. "Y'all together?"

"No!" I answered.

"Maybe. Why?" Zak spoke over me.

"Boy, don't tell that lie," I nearly yelled.

"So, there's nothing between us. That's the lie you wanna tell?"

"Zak, seriously?" I asked, waiting for him to take it back. I stared at him, hoping he'd read that this was not the time nor the place for this.

Everyone's eyes were on the two of us. Zak bobbed his head. "You're so quick to call me childish, but you were all in my—"

"Nope! Not doing it. I'm out. I had a great time with everyone except this asshole. I will see you later, Nelle." I gave her a hug and grabbed my keys. Trevor asked if I was okay, but Zakari answered for me and followed me out the door.

I walked with a purpose to the parking lot, ignoring him the entire way. I had no intention of engaging with his big stupid ass until he blocked me from my car.

"Gia, hold up!"

"Fuck you, Zakari. I can't believe you did that in there. We ain't did nothing but kiss and your immature ass acting like I belong to you."

"I'm sorry. I was trippin'. You were all over that nigga in my face. What did you expect?"

"For you to mind your damn business! What does any of that have to do with you?"

"Nothing." He tapped his fist on my car. "You right, nothing at all. Based on how you operate, you need to leave him alone. That's Cam's friend. You can't do him like you do other niggas."

"Exactly how do I do it, Zak? Since you know me so damn well."

Zak's head fell back, and he looked to the heavens. His deep breaths made me nervous. My eyes followed the rise and fall of his chest as he leaned against my car door. Wanting to jump on him right now confused the shit out of me. Yes, the man was beyond sexy, but his ass was not for me. Being Janelle's brother complicated things. His temper and jealousy made it worse.

Why couldn't my panties stay dry around him?

"Let's go somewhere real quick."

"Zakari," I whined. He didn't get it.

"Gia, please. I'm sorry. I was acting like a kid. I can't seem to think about anything else but being with you and the shit is fucking with me. I want you to see me as some thing other than your best friend's brother. That's the problem, right?"

"Nothing is going to change that, Zakari."

"Will you at least come with me?"

That damn question could go two ways and my mind imagined the gutter version. "Fine."

Zak placed his hand on my hip and pulled me toward him. I halfway resisted. He pressed his lips together and slowly exhaled. "Gia, come here."

I listened and got closer. Zak wrapped his arms around my waist, resting his hands at the small of my back. "I'm sorry." He gazed into my eyes until I lowered my head.

"Okay." That one word came out soft and sweet. Didn't even sound like me.

He pulled me up against his erection. "See what you do to me."

If only I could do something with that thing. I backed away before my ass got caught up. Not happening.

We got in our cars, and he led the way.

# THIRTEEN

## Gianna

"Shit!" Zak had pulled into the parking lot of a bar I'd frequented in the past couple of weeks.

Zak found a close spot and let me take it. I waited in the car until he parked. He opened my door for me to get out. "A bar?"

"What? You expected me to take you home? 'Cause we can do that, too."

I nudged his chest. "Shut up. That's not what I meant." Yes, it was. It was exactly what I'd wanted.

As soon as we walked inside, I scanned the room quickly, ensuring I didn't recognize anyone.

We sat at the end of the bar. Zak faced me on his stool. "What do you want to drink?"

"See if they can make Angry Balls."

Zak dipped his chin. "Nah, you can ask that shit." We laughed until a cute girl asked for our alcoholic desires.

The bartender chuckled at my request, but she knew what it was. She got points for that. Zak received his draft, Blue Moon.

"Eww! That stuff tastes like perfume and oranges. How do you drink that?"

"Ay, you just worry about downing them balls."

My jaw dropped before I punched him in the arm. "Nasty ass."

"You have no idea." He winked. His ass had better stop messing with me.

I gave my attention to my drink for a few moments. When I closed my eyes for too long, Zak placed his hand on my knee. "You okay, G?"

"Uh, yeah. A little tired." Yeah, right. I was briefly daydreaming about how he'd feel on me, in me, and everything else nasty.

"We won't stay too long." Zak sat back a little but still faced me. "What's been up with you? Besides delaying the inevitable."

"Inevitable?"

"You and me."

"Yeah, okay, little boy."

He nodded slowly. "Keep playing. You gon' find out."

"No, the hell I won't. We can't."

"Man, we can do whatever the fuck we want. We grown. Why you so hard up about being with me? What's the worst that can happen?"

I could hate it. I could like it or even love it. Love it too damn much. I didn't want to get caught up with anyone I wouldn't be able to avoid afterward.

"Doesn't matter." I shrugged.

"Guess you back on your Tinder account. Or whatever the fuck else you use." He scoffed.

"Shut up. For your info, I uninstalled the app because of you."

Zak's head tilted to the side like I was lying, so I pulled out my phone and showed him. "Good for you."

"Still seeing D'Mario?"

"Nigga, why you asking all these questions?"

"My bad. You right. Not my business." He gulped the rest of his beer and ordered another one. "Gia, I want you. Your lips only made me more curious about the rest of you. How do I get in? If his punk ass got in, why can't I?"

I chewed on that question. I cared about Zak. I cared about his feelings in a way that threw flags whenever I fantasized being with him. How was one kiss that damn powerful? It pulled at me too, but I found ways around it.

"You're Janelle's—"

"Brother! Okay! What else you got? That's not cutting it."

"I see you different, that's all. You aren't, as you say, some random nigga. So, after the sun comes up, I have to be around you. That's awkward. Shit, things are weird now all because of one damn kiss."

He poked his lips out. "It's only weird because you won't let your guard down. I want to see you. I want to take on your battles alongside you. I want to protect you from your fears." He laughed at my lips twisted to the side. "Yeah, I want your body too, but that's not the only reason I'm here. What you've done before with other dudes is your business, but what I want from you...with you...is something completely different."

"That's the problem. You want something I'm not willing to give anyone."

"That's why you got this done?" He grabbed my left hand and traced his finger on the tattoo on my wrist. It read "No Love" because I meant it and never wanted to forget it. I got it done soon after Momma died. I pulled my hand back. "Gia, you don't have to go through life afraid of being loved."

"I'm not. I just don't believe in it. At least not for me."

"So, in your mind, no one could ever love you?" He sounded like Janelle sitting in his chair. No one had to understand my choices, but they needed to respect them and leave me the hell alone about it. "Gia, I'm not tryna piss you off or anything. I see you don't wanna talk about this so I'll drop it."

I nodded and finished my Angry Balls. Zak appeared defeated. My attraction to him was evident, but this push-back deserved an explanation. I respected him enough to give him one.

After ordering another drink and some loaded nachos, I gave Zak the rundown of my family's history with trifling ass men. I protected my heart above all else. Yeah, I might go through life missing out on what others thought was worth it, but heartbreak from any man wouldn't be a part of my life's story ever again. I was perfectly content with it, but I got tired of asking everyone else to accept it.

Zak listened to my story and promised he wouldn't put me through any of what Blair had done to my mom or my grandfather to Mimi. I left out the part where I tried to be with someone before.

In college, Alex Brooks was my first love. I thought I'd won over the curse in my family. We were together for seven months and had said the l-word. Alex was it for me. I imagined the wedding, the kids, and the happily ever after. I was even ready to tell Momma about him. If we'd made it to a year, I promised I'd tell her.

Alex was two years older than me and had an off-campus apartment. I went to his place to make dinner for him one night. When I'd knocked, another woman answered in a damn sheer robe. When I got loud, Alex appeared behind her and told me he wasn't really feeling me anymore. Those were his exact words, and that nigga closed the door in my face.

I didn't get back at him the way I'd wanted because I got the call that Momma was sick the following week. My life still hadn't recovered from two back-to-back blows. Obviously, everything with my mom trumped a little heart-crack.

All I'd learned was that Momma was right about men and I shouldn't have tried to prove her wrong. My distraction with Alex made me miss the fact that my mother was slowly dying. She'd said nothing to me. I'd never asked, even when I'd noticed her weight-loss and fatigued-filled eyes whenever we video-chatted.

"I don't know who screwed up generations before me, but they really ruined it for all of us."

"A family curse? You sure that's true?"

"How else would you explain it?"

He leaned back and pondered for a moment. "Bad luck, I guess."

"So, you don't believe in generational curses?"

"I do. That shit is real. Your situation may be a string of poor judgment. Good love exists all around you. Why would it skip you? You are an amazing woman. Any man can see that. If you're going around picking a D'Mario over a Zakari, it'll feel like an unfortunate cycle."

I laughed out loud at his conclusion. "So, it's our fault for trusting someone who showed genuine interest and then dropped us? Not D'Mario, but in general."

He shook his head, then raised both hands in surrender. "This feels like a trap."

"Zak, for real. I want to know how you really feel."

"Look, Gia, I am not coming down on what you think is

going on. I think y'all should've tried harder. The first go-round didn't work. Okay! Try again. Don't spread a lie about love not being possible in one family on the entire planet. It sounds crazy. Someone existed for each woman who believed this lie and passed it down. She chose not to give it a chance and now all of you have suffered believing that shit."

Each word stung, and I wanted to slap him. I hoped he choked on the loaded nacho chip he threw in his mouth. On the one hand, I felt stupid because he had a point. Hell, he had a few. Then again, he'd called the women in my family crazy. That's what I heard.

Right before I'd was about to give him an earful, someone tapped my arm. "Eve?"

# FOURTEEN

# Gianna

My shoulders dropped at his voice. Troy was the reason I'd searched the space when we first walked in. "Heyyy!" I turned my body completely away from Zak.

"I thought that was you." Troy was the type of cute I hated to like. The light-bright mofos with curly hair. His curls were cut short. His plump pink lips thinned as a smile that drew a slight drip from me spread across his face. "Whatchu up to tonight? I'm free if you wanna come through."

"Wow!" Zak dragged the word on the other side of me.

"That's you?" Troy asked low enough for only me to hear him.

"No, but I am busy tonight."

"Cool. Hit me up whenever, I can knock those kinks out. You look tense." He winked at me and walked away.

When I got the guts to face Zak, he had already stood up. He went through his wallet and placed cash on the counter after he got the bartender's attention. She asked if he needed a receipt. He declined and took off.

I followed him out the door. "Zak?" His strides were

long compared to mine. I had to jog to catch up. "Zak? Really? What are you mad about now?"

"I ain't. I got shit to do." He didn't slow down for nothing. We reached his already unlocked car.

"Wait! Why are you leaving like this?"

"Gia, don't play dumb. Or should I say Eve? That's the second nigga calling you that. If I didn't know any better, I'd think you were a pro with yo' fake name and shit."

"You know damn well I ain't no damn prostitute."

He scoffed. "I don't know shit. Every time you in public, another nigga you fucked pops up. A good nigga wants you, but you'd rather sell yourself for—"

"Fuck you, Zakari. Don't get mad at me for being just like you. I can fuck whoever I want. You ain't my man. I don't say shit about you and your hoes."

"I don't have hoes. The women I deal with are honest about what they want and who they are. They don't hide behind bullshit curses to avoid feeling anything for anybody."

I rushed off to my car. I sat there, taking breaths deep enough to not cry. It didn't work.

Who cared what Zakari thought of me?

Shit, I did. I shouldn't, but dammit, I did.

My head fell onto the headrest as my breathing slowed. I jumped when someone knocked on my passenger window. Zak motioned for me to unlock the door. I smacked my lips and sat back. His ass could stay outside.

"Gia, open the door."

I rolled my eyes. What were we doing? We were fighting and had done nothing but kiss once. He wasn't mine and I wasn't his. Yet, we fought with enough emotion for a stranger to assume more had happened between us.

Zak opened the door after I unlocked it. A quick swipe

across my face was all I had time to do before he sat in the car. He left the door open with one foot outside. "G, why are you crying?"

I shrugged and stared outside my window to avoid his eyes.

We both sat in silence for almost a minute. "I didn't mean what I said. This ain't even me. I don't know what it is about you. As a kid, I tripped on how beautiful and funny you were. Now, it seems like I have more respect for you than you do for yourself."

"What?" I whipped my neck his way.

"That didn't come out right. I mean, I want you to have the best of what a man can give you. I hate that you don't want it. You deserve the world, but you're settling for whatever the hell you're doing."

"Sounds like you're only mad I won't sleep with you."

"Miss me with that, Gia. It's more than about sex."

"You were all 'let me handle that for you. If you only want sex, I can do that.' Now, how I live my life is a problem for you. Well, guess what? It's *my* life and how you perceive it is your problem. Not mine."

"So, now I can't care?"

"Ay, Eve! Don't forget to call me!" Troy and some guys walked past my car, being loud as hell. His friends laughed as he yelled that shit.

Zak tensed up, but I was so grateful he didn't react. "That's the disrespect you want? Niggas calling you out?"

"No, I—"

"You said you quit that app."

"I did. I met him here a couple weeks ago."

"Damn, Gia! You really out here just giving it away to whoever asks, but I'm the one you reject. That's some bullshit."

"They don't mean shit to me. But you! You have the power to hurt me in ways they can't."

"I wouldn't."

"You can't be sure of that."

"Neither can you. I don't want a good time with you, Gia. I want a life with you."

I smacked my lips. "How are you so sure of what you want? You're too fucking childish to understand anything."

His head jerked back. "Nigga, you the one to talk. You're the one looking at life from a childish perspective."

"So, you really tryna get slapped tonight, huh? Keep on talking to me crazy, Zak. Keep on."

"Look, I'm sorry, but this shit is frustrating. You don't —" His phone rang, and when he pulled it out, there was a half-naked female on the ID. I couldn't make out the name since I didn't want to make it obvious I was being nosy.

He rejected the call. I pointed at his phone. "Don't you have to take that? I'm positive your sure-of-what-they-want hoes need your attention tonight."

Zak snorted and nodded. "I might as well go. We ain't getting nowhere, anyway."

"Nowhere to get, bruh. You want me to be something I'm not."

He rolled his eyes. "Yeah, okay. Just protect yourself, a'ight."

"I always do."

Zak stared at me, squinting like he could reach me through his eyes. When that failed, he dropped his head and smiled. "You are so fucking hardheaded."

I laughed at his defeat. My head was made of stone when I made up my mind. "That's 'cause you keep trying to control me."

"Nah, that ain't it. I want you to be you. And to be happy."

"Who said I wasn't, Zakari?"

"You! If you were so damn secure, you'd stop fighting me. Let me show you something different."

"Boy, shut up." I rolled my eyes and folded my arms over my lap. He acted as if he had all the answers to questions I'd never asked. Zak leaned over the center console. "What are you doing?" I kept the distance between us, pressing against his chest.

"Come here." His voice was breathy, an almost whisper. *Who did he think he was?*

My brow cocked for two seconds, but his tongue swiping my bottom lip pulled me in submission. I moved closer to him and closed my eyes.

Zak's wet lips pressed against mine and removed all my inhibitions. I told myself we weren't going there, but he so easily overtook me. A minute ago, I'd wanted to curse him out. Now, I'd do him right in this front seat and not give a damn who saw us.

I gave him my tongue, slipping it between his lips. His mouth devoured mine. If this was a contest, his ass won. That tongue of his explored my mouth as if looking for a hidden treasure. Once my moans released, I had to break away.

"Dammit, Zak." I barely got out. "Why you gotta do stuff like that?"

"What? You can't handle a little boy kissing you?"

"Ha, ha. Whatever." I leaned back, trying not to squirm in my seat. Holding back this urge wasn't normal for me. The shit was more challenging than I'd imagined. "Get out of my car before we do something we will regret."

Zak sucked his teeth. "I ain't gon' regret nothing. Shit,

neither will you. Trust me." He placed his hand on my thigh, too close to my goods.

"Boy, go!" I pushed his hand away. He laughed, but I was serious.

"A'ight. Promise me something though."

"What now?"

"Consider what I said. Give us a chance. Leave all them trash niggas behind. If I can't please you, I won't make it awkward. I'll understand and be mature about us. I'm saying, I am the only mature one in here, anyway."

I hit his arm. "I'll see."

"You'll see?" he asked.

"Yeah, I might have to call someone up to finish what you started." He glared at me with a raised brow. "Damn! Okay. I'll think about it."

"Do that." That man got in my face and tugged my bottom lip with his teeth. He'd crossed lines drawn for any guy I dealt with. My ass liked it.

Zakari broke down parts of my wall with a smile, a wink, and mind-blowing mouth-to-mouth action. Anything further would be game over for me. I knew it, felt it. We had to stay away from each other. I'd let him hope for now.

## FIFTEEN

# Zakari



"Y'all just talked?"

"Yes, damn. Why you keep asking the same thing?" My sister popped up on me days after her game night. I'd already texted her my apology that night and the following day. I could admit I'd come out of pocket.

"Because Gia said the same thing."

"The truth works like that, J." I folded the basketball shorts in my hand while she flipped through my hundreds-of-useless-channels cable package.

"Like hell it does. Not with you two. Especially with your little tantrum. Tell the truth and shame the devil. What is going on between you and Gia?"

"Nothing but two adults having a conversation."

"About?"

"Damn, you nosy."

She pointed her middle finger at me. "Zakari Jarell Lawrence! Answer the question."

"Not my whole name." I cracked up at her steaming scowl, stacking the undershirt on a neat pile next to me.

"Why you so bothered, sis? Pretty boy didn't get his date? That's why you here?"

"See? That's what I'm talking about. Why are *you* so bothered about Trevor? That's the real question." Janelle set the remote on the table and got up. "If nothing was going on, you wouldn't sound jealous. Are you jealous that someone else might want your girl?"

"She ain't my girl. Stop being messy."

"Mmmhmm. Something's going on more than talking and I will find out."

"Do your best."

She disappeared to the back of my apartment. I thought she was going through my bedroom until the toilet flushed. A minute later, she was back in my face.

"You lucky I have stuff to do today. Trust, I will find out if either of you are lying to me."

"Why you even care? Not that there's anything to care about. Why you doing all this?"

She lowered herself into the same spot as before. "Zakari, Gia is convinced that she'll never be in love because of some nonsense her mom and grandmother told her. Rest in peace, Mimi and Miss Elaine. The girl won't let anyone in and that's all crap. Trevor might change her mind. She needs to live and love. Make mistakes. Find the right one and have a family. The girl is lonely. Everyone she loved from birth is gone. I don't want her believing opinions instead of facts."

"Yeah, she mentioned the so-called family curse. She has to learn her own way, though. You can't force dudes on her and pray they fix what *you* see as a problem."

"You don't?"

I shrugged. Gia had a lot going on with missing the ladies who raised her and thinking her dad represented the type of man she'd fall for. He was the present factor that kept her in her head. Nothing I said made her see things differently. She only understood one type of relationship. The one she had with that clown at the club and the other one at the bar.

Gia could do better than both of them and whoever else she'd been with. We were still young, but even I accepted that one day there'd be something better to look forward to. A forever-type thing. I'd had my fun and still did. My needs and wants would change in the future and I'd probably be corny in love like my parents.

I assumed I'd possibly want that in a few years, but having the chance at the one woman I categorized as "keep dreaming, nigga" sped things up for me. Ain't like if I got in we'd say vows. Got to start somewhere, though.

"Not my business, Janelle. She's not my girl, remember?"

"I hate you so much right now. You're hiding something."

"All I'm doing is folding clothes. Didn't you say you had shit to do? Go do it. I'm busy."

Janelle smacked her lips and rose from the couch for the last time, I hoped. She dragged her feet to the door and held onto the knob. When my sister turned around, I read her mind since I'd done the same shit to her too many times.

"J, go! Don't even try it." I stretched my arm out to protect the clothes sitting next to me on the sofa.

"Ugh, you suck." She faced the door to leave, then quickly ran to where I sat, picked up the folded clothes, and threw them.

"Dammit, J!" I couldn't help but laugh when she bellowed a good one.

"Payback, you bastard. Love you," she finished in a

high-pitched voice like she didn't just waste ten minutes of good folding.

The door slammed behind her as she ran out.

---

Byron knocked on the door. He'd texted, telling me he was outside. I opened the door for him. "Another night off the leash and so soon from the last one? You must be in trouble."

"Ahh, shut that shit up. I'll gladly wear a leash to have what I have." He came inside and shut the door. "Can't even get through the threshold before such spewed hatred. You will soon find the one who'd make you want to chill too."

"You would say some weak shit like that." We laughed on the way to the sofa. "There's beer in the fridge if you want any."

We were meeting up with a couple of friends from college in a little over an hour. Byron wanted to chill at the house beforehand for a quick game of 2K20.

When it came out, it had me more hyped at Tobe Nwigwe on the soundtrack. He was Houston to the fullest, repping the southwest like the true legend he was on his way to becoming. He was a force to be reckoned with. Plus, he didn't rap about the foolishness that most of the industry did.

There were a handful of artists I rocked with and they were all vets. Blame my pops for that one. All he played was '90s hip-hop. I grew up appreciating true lyrical gifts. My generation had a few in the mix, but the majority I wasn't rocking with.

I finally filled Byron in on the Gia situation. He got too

excited that I even cared about someone.

"How are you still be clownin' me about Trina?"

"I said I like the woman. We ain't nothin' like y'all."

"Shit, not yet. It's only a matter of time."

"Did you not hear me say she won't let me in?"

He chuckled. "I did. I'm sure she'll come around. Show up for her when she doesn't even know she needs it."

"How? She talks to me about personal shit, but if I try to get close in a genuine way, she shoots me down."

"Probably 'cause she knows you a hoe."

"Ay, she gets it in as much as I do. She keep trippin' about me being her best friend's brother. I can't change that."

Byron twisted his mouth, brooding on a solution, I guessed. "Okay. Does she like music?"

"What the hell does that have—"

"If you answer the question, I can tell you. She got you all snappy and shit. You need to get that taken care of fast."

"Man, shut up. I guess she does. Who doesn't like music?"

"True. So, when I was tryna get with Trina, I used to text her songs. It gotta be shit women like. Or at least something Gia will like."

"Sounds a'ight. I'll see."

"You're an R&B man. I'm sure you can think of some songs to tell her how you feel better than you can. Be clever with it. I'm telling you; they love that shit."

I got a call from Josh, telling me our usual bowling alley had their league night tonight. No room for us amateurs. Plans changed to meet at Main Event in the Fountains in Stafford. We headed out as soon as the call ended.

At Main Event, Josh and Gerald had already put our names on the list. The wait was long enough to eat first, which I was always down for. It took about five minutes to find a table big enough for the four of us. We ordered right away.

Halfway through my Wild West Burger, my attention hooked onto a familiar face coming my way. *Fuck!*

"Hey stranger!" Myesha stopped next to me. She tapped the outside of my thigh under the table.

"What's up? What you doing here?" The guys all shared that same expression. No one knew who she was and I had no plans on filling them in.

"Here with some girlfriends. Where you been?" She settled closer to me, rubbing my thigh, getting within reach of my dick.

I didn't see her outside a hotel building or the gym, so all this shit she did was new. Myesha kept biting the corner of her lip. Her voice sounded needy.

"Busy."

"Too busy for..." She finally acknowledged the guys at the table with a wave. "Can we talk for a minute?"

Byron gave me a side-eye. I'd deal with him later.

I wiped my hands with a napkin and told the guys I'd be back. Myesha led me past what I assumed was a group of her friends since they watched us with grins too big for what this really was. Not a damn thing.

We stood near the entrance next to the billiards area. I widened my stance and stood firm with my arms crossed. Myesha wasn't about to make this appear to be anything more than the truth.

"Why are you dodgin' me, Zak? You with somebody?"

I snorted. "Stop actin' like you waitin' on me, Myesha. You still wit yo' man."

She sucked her teeth. "That ain't stop you before. Kitty needs her Zaky."

Myesha was a regular girl. Sexy, but regular. A dime a dozen. The constant texting and calling turned me off which made me blow her off more than once. My others understood the need to chill. She grabbed my hands and wrapped them around her. I pulled away, but not quick enough.

"Zak?" Janelle's voice came out of nowhere. I turned to find she wasn't alone.

Gia's brows hiked as she pressed her lips together. It didn't take a genius to decipher what that meant.

"H-Hey." I had nothing else.

Janelle's eyes widened as Gia's avoided mine. "So, little brother, is this your girl?"

"Nah!"

"Yes!" Myesha answered, but louder than me. I could tell the women heard me, too. Both of them squinted at us.

"Well, which is it? Never mind, I'm Janelle. Zak's sister." She offered her hand to Myesha, and this girl took it like this shit was normal.

"Janelle!" Myesha squealed. "I've heard so much about you. It's so great to finally meet you." The hell was she talking about? I had never talked about my family with her let alone mentioned I had a sister. Who the fuck was she fronting for?

"Ay, your friends are over there waiting for you," I reminded her.

Myesha smacked her lips and tapped my chest. "They can wait, baby. I want to meet your people."

Gia's gaze burned a hole through me. Her eyes went down to the hooking of Myesha's arm in mine. I'd been so distracted that I didn't notice it. I took a step to the side to break away.

"I'm Myesha. A really, *really* good friend of Zaky."

"Zaky?" Gia barely held in her irritation behind her forced half-smile.

"It's not what you think," I tried to clarify to Gia.

She shook her head. "I don't think anything, Zakari." Gia turned to Myesha. "Nice to see Zaky here has someone special in his life."

Myesha smiled with what resembled pride. I wanted to stop her immediately, but cussing her ass out wouldn't have been a good look.

"Yeah, it's been a few months. He's been good to me."

Gia's head jerked back. "Wow! That long? How freaking amazing!" She put on a show with her hand on her chest and her mouth opened.

"Oh! Um, that's good to hear." Janelle narrowed her eyes at me again. For a second, I thought she saw through the bullshit.

When I had Gia's attention, I shook my head and hoped she understood. By the cocked brow and lips pursed to the side, she didn't. I felt like I'd gotten caught cheating. My palms were all sweaty and shit.

Gia wanted to say something. I knew she did. Maybe even wanted to put her hands on me opposite of the way I'd wanted her to.

*Fuck!*

What was this woman doing? Gia's wall was already a challenge without her ever meeting anybody from my life. Myesha was nothing but an occasional fuck. This stunt she pulled came at the worst time.

"Sorry, Myesha. We didn't know Zak ever took someone seriously. That's why we're surprised." Janelle attempted to explain the awkward silence.

"I understand. He hasn't met my daughter yet, but with the way he treats me, it might be soon."

"Daughter? You've really been holding out." Janelle's voice hiked. "What else do we not know?"

"A'ight, that's enough, Myesha. You taking this shit too far," I warned through my gritted teeth. "This is my family. Just stop."

Gia screwed her face before that slow nod. "Family. Yep, that's it. I'm happy for you and your man. You look good together."

"Very cute," Janelle added. "Well, let us get out of your way. Have fun!"

Myesha's smile stretched ear to ear and that shit got deep under my skin. Gia and Janelle walked away.

I faced Myesha. "What the fuck was that? Why you lying?"

"That's what you get for ducking me. That Gia girl ain't no damn family." Her brow furrowed as her eyes followed my sister and Gia to the line.

"How would you know? You don't know shit about me and now you got my sister thinking we're together. I don't play games like that. Lose my fucking number." I should've told her ass that weeks ago. Running into her man at the gym from time to time had my ass paranoid. I wasn't trying to fight a nigga over no chick that I didn't give a fuck about.

Myesha caught my arm. "Wait! I'm sorry. Don't be mad at me."

"I'd have to care to be mad." I left her with that to obsess over.

The guys were heading my way after I only took a few steps from Myesha. "Our lane is ready," Gerald informed me. "Trouble in paradise?"

Josh laughed. "Gotta be. Your girl looks like she's about to cry."

"Man, she ain't nothing to me."

"Does she know that?" Gerald asked. I didn't look her way. Whatever she felt was on her.

Byron returned to the group after speaking to Janelle in the line. "So, that's Gia?"

Josh stopped in the line for shoes. "Who? I thought ol' girl was Myesha."

I didn't answer since they were about to walk right past us. Janelle greeted the group with a wave but continued with Gia to wherever they were going.

Byron's worried face let me know where I stood. We could talk about it without the guys. I'd get my earful on the way back to my apartment for sure. Maybe he'd have an idea for me to get on Gia's good side.

Watching those black skinny jeans hug Gia's ass on the way to the bar had me on pause. I wanted her to turn around for only a second. She didn't.

Myesha walked past me and interrupted my view. Her group of friends all looked at me crazy, but the way she looked at Gia pulled at me. She'd try some foul shit. I was now aware of that side of her. She glared at Gia too hard for me to do nothing.

We gave our shoe sizes to the teen behind the counter. After I got them, I handed mine to Byron and told him I'd be right back.

"Do what you gotta do. Fix that shit." Byron nodded.

"If I don't come back before my turn, y'all play it." He dapped me and I began my stroll to Janelle and Gia. They stood near the bar, waiting for a couple of seats.

I passed the group of women who must've known what I said to their girl Myesha. The closer I got to Gia, the warmer my armpits heated.

This could only go a couple of ways. I had an idea which was more likely and braced myself.

# SIXTEEN

# Gianna

Someone grabbed at my waist. I flew around to see who had the balls to touch me like that. Janelle jumped at my quick spin.

Of course, it was Zak's ass. "What are you doing?"

"Lemme talk to you," he said.

Janelle pursed her lips. "Mmmhmm. Y'all negroes shole do a lot of talking."

"We have nothing to talk about, Zakari. Your girl is watching me, so walk away."

"Oh, please. That girl ain't gonna do nothing." Janelle made sure Myesha saw us watching her watch us with a wave.

"We don't want Zaky's girl thinking anything is going on here with his family. She looks concerned." I locked eyes with him.

"Gia, let me talk to you, please."

"Talk, fam." I folded my arms across my chest, waiting for him to explain that shit. Janelle's nosy behind read all the tension. His ass might say something stupid.

"Y'all might not be screwing, but y'all doing something." Janelle pointed at both of us with narrowed eyes.

Zak gave me puppy dog eyes. His big ass shouldn't be out here making that damn face. Poking out his lip only made me want to bite it. I rolled my eyes before agreeing to talk. We walked over to the arcade area for some privacy from Janelle.

"Gia, let me explain." He started right away.

"You sure your girl will be okay with that? She doesn't appear too happy with you talking with me."

"She's not my—"

"You fucking her, right?"

"Gia, let's not—"

"Answer me, Zakari!" My blood boiled as if the answer mattered. He wasn't my man. Even so, his pursuit of me made me feel some type of way if he had a woman. The way she told it; they were a thing.

"Yes, but not—"

"So, we have nothing to—"

"Would you let me finish a fucking sentence!" This nigga raised his voice at me. The people nearby briefly gave us their attention. I heard an "Oooh, she in trouble" somewhere in the crowd.

"G, I'm sorry. You ain't listening. She made all that shit up. We fucked around a bit, but I ain't seen her in weeks. Everyone that hit me up since I tasted your lips got curved. I only want you. I mean that shit."

"Why would you do that? We ain't doing nothing, anyway. We family."

"Come on, bruh. I was trying to get her off our trail."

"There's no trail. There's nothing." I released a long breath with his eyes on me. "To think I actually believed you. Shit, you made me almost give a damn about—" I shrugged with no interest in even going there with him. "Whatever, it doesn't matter."

I started my way back to Janelle. Zak grabbed my arm and pulled me back to him. "No! I'm not done." He spun me around, so we were face to face. "Please don't let this bullshit get in the way. I want you, Gia. That has to mean something."

I took two steps back and bumped into a wall. Nowhere to go, Zak pressed his body against mine like no one could see us. With each of his hands on my hips, he leaned in and brushed his lips over mine. "I want you so fucking bad. Let's leave right now so I can show you."

The room became blurry. Dizzied by this level of horniness had me uneasy. "S-Stop. We ain't going nowhere." I pushed him off. If he could feel my heart racing and panties almost leaking, he'd know I wanted anything but for him to stop. "Zakari, this is wrong."

"Miss me with that shit, Gia. You're hardheaded as fuck."

"Maybe."

"Let me come over later at least."

"Hell, no. Go to your girl's place. I'm not fuckin' with you. I ain't tryna be in your rotation."

"You don't listen. I told you I shut all that down."

"I don't believe you. Your word don't go that far with me. You're still a man. A liar."

"If she was mine, I'd be there with her and not with you."

Zak moved in closer, causing me to hold my breath for a few moments. "I gotta go. Janelle is waiting on me." I moved around him and sped up when he tried to stop me again.

Janelle held my seat at the bar. She had a tall glass full of some blue drink in front of her.

"I ordered an appetizer combo," she said when I moved her purse from the chair beside her to sit.

"Thank you, girl."

Janelle showed me what she had ordered on the menu before she faced me, waiting for me to say something.

"Oooh, that looks good." I brought the menu up to my face and between us to block her glare.

"So you really not gonna tell me what's going on between you and my brother."

"Nothing to tell."

"Oh, chick, you must think I'm crazy. All this energy between y'all is not nothing. I should leave yo' ass here and have him drive you home since y'all best friends now."

"I'd get an Uber. What else you got?"

She shoved me and laughed. "I hate you. At least give me a heads up before you become my sister-in-law."

"Whoa, whoa, whoa. Ain't nobody said no shit like that. We only—" I stopped myself.

Janelle yelped. "You what, Gia? Tell me!"

The bartender came over and took my drink order. They had so much fruity stuff that might be tasty. I randomly chose one.

"It's not that serious. I only kissed—No! He kissed me."

She gasped and cheesed like a damn kid. "I knew it! I knew it!"

"You knew what, crazy?"

"That you liked him. My brother done growed up." She laughed. "Enough to have your ass bothered. How was it?"

Her silly ass wanted details? Who asked that about their brother? I didn't give her a damn thing. My drink came in time to change the subject. She wouldn't let it go for a minute, but when I asked about Cameron, her eyes lit up, and her mouth started running.

In the middle of eating, it was our turn to bowl. The bartender said to take the food with us.

After getting our shoes, we found our lane. That motherfucker had to be right next to Zakari and his friends. Janelle cackled when we were literally in the same seating area. Some bullshit! He paid somebody to put us here. Had to. Then again, my luck had always sucked.

I tried to ignore them, but that shit was a struggle with his eyes on me the entire time. Zak's eyes begged for me to meet them. *Nope*!

Once I successfully ignored Zakari's staring, I noticed this damn area was full of groups of fine-ass men. With D'Mario and Troy out of the picture, I needed a replacement. A few of them were on my radar.

I removed my jean jacket, revealing my fitted top underneath. The few extra eyes worked to my advantage. Even caught two of Zak's friends watching me. All that bending over more than I needed or sticking my ass out for the onlookers wasn't my thing. It never took more than being myself for the welcomed attention.

"Damn, girl!" The one named Josh said when I hit my third strike. They were all flukes. I bowled okay. Better than some, worse than most. Tonight made me seem pretty good.

Zak cut his eyes his friend's way. He dared not to say anything. Whoever wanted to celebrate my bowling, body, or anything else could do so if I said so. I wouldn't be that cold and go after his friend, but a little flirting wouldn't hurt.

"You do this a lot?" Josh asked.

"I do a little."

"I bet." He leaned back on the couch.

I giggled enough to annoy Zak. "I'm not trying that hard. It's only working out that way."

"That's probably the story of your life, huh? You don't look like the type that has to work too hard for what she wants." Once he flashed his smile, I did the same.

"Josh! Your turn." Zak's attitude wasn't discreet.

I rolled my eyes at him. He sat there with his hands clasped while leaning forward the whole time. He'd bowl and come back to the same position. He pulled out his phone and completely spaced out from the rest of us.

Janelle sparked up a conversation with Byron. They seemed familiar with each other. He kept checking on Zak, which was weird. As nosy and crazy as Janelle was before, she acted like nothing had happened between Zak and me. Hell, so did I.

The waitress passed by and I got her attention to order another drink. Josh walked up to us. "Hey, I can pay for her tab," he told the girl.

"Nah, it's taken care of." We all turned to Zak.

"You don't have to. I can pay my—"

"It's already taken care of." He stood to bowl his turn.

The woman left with my order. We were there for an hour and so were the guys. When I beat Janelle three times in a row, our time was up.

"Where y'all going after this?" Josh asked me.

"Nigga, why you asking?" Zak countered.

"'Cause I am. What's the problem?" Josh came back at Zak with the same amount of irritation.

"Laser tag," I yelled to break their gaze from each other. "We paid for one game there. That's it."

"Sounds fun. Who's down for laser tag?" Josh asked the other two guys, completely disregarding Zak.

Everyone but Zak agreed to play with us. Janelle pulled him to the side since we were in their lane, waiting for the last frame. Whatever she told him had him constantly rolling his eyes.

When Gerald finished, the game ended, and we all headed to the laser tag line. Zak went to the bar instead. I didn't see his girl anywhere. Byron joined Zak, leaving only four of us.

Josh didn't say too much after he felt the heat from Zak, but we still had fun teaming against Gerald and Janelle. Gerald scored the highest. His quiet behind was picking off the kids most of the time.

We came out and I checked my phone. It was on silent the whole time. I had four missed texts from Zak.

*Songs? Why the hell would he send me songs?* I ignored them since I didn't have time to listen here. As I looked up from my phone, his eyes were on me again. Byron stood next to him, waiting near the dining area.

Janelle and I told everyone goodbye before finally leaving. Janelle filled me in on the conversation with her brother. She told him to calm down, then she threw me under the bus. Zak's intentions wouldn't get fulfilled by me.

After she finished for the millionth time trying to change me, I put in my headphones. Just one side to see what Zak sent. He had the nerve to text me songs about being sorry. He did him and I'd continue doing me. No hard feelings.

What the hell did I expect from him? No love. I needed to remind myself daily because he got close to making me think that maybe what I felt about him meant something. I kept seeing his stupid eyes searching mine, then smiling like he found something to smile about in me.

"Gia?" I shook in my seat. I listened to the music with only the right bud in my ear. It wasn't enough to stay in the conversation.

"Huh?"

"What are you doing?"

"Nothing. What?"

"I asked about Trevor."

"What about him? Didn't you text me his number yesterday?"

"Yes, and he's still waiting."

"I ain't about to call nobody. Trevor's a no-go."

She sucked her teeth. "Every damn man is a no-go. You might as well go lesbian. That way you won't have to worry about that stupid curse crap."

"Oh, now you tryna get thrown out of your own car."

"Heifer, I'm the one driving."

"I ain't jumping. So, you'd be the one in the street. I'd manage."

"You're crazy and you are not getting off that easy with me."

"When has it ever been that easy with you? Nelle, I told you where I stand. Going back and forth with you is stupid, and it's getting on my damn nerves."

"I don't care! Somebody needs to say something to you about it. Your mom told you what she thought based on her own experience. You are not your mother, Gia."

"I didn't say I was."

"Then what do you want to be?"

"What?"

"Forget about what your mother taught you and be honest about what Gia wants. Do you really want to be so hard against men because of what other women went through?"

"I don't want to make the same mistakes and get hurt."

"This is your life. Live that shit full out. Let go of the things you were taught if they don't make you better. No offense, but 'never fall in love' is a shit lesson. Just like you are a good woman, there are good men out there. Every man is not your dad or your grandfather or whoever else made the women in your family hate love."

"They didn't hate love. They were simply protecting me from possible heartbreak. What if I trust a man with my heart and then he decides he no longer wants me? I'd be right where they were, especially if a kid's involved."

"There are more sides to a what if, G. That could happen to anyone. Or the one with your heart could guard it with his life and make sure he'd never hurt you. Those men exist. There isn't only one type. If that were the case, every woman would be alone. But it simply isn't true.

"A few rotten apples ended up in your family tree. So what? Create your own story. Fall in love and let it take you places you didn't think possible. If it doesn't work, try again. You will find what makes you happy because there's no way what you're doing now is working for you. I know it's not."

After Alex, I didn't dare try to go against my teachings to never trust men. I believed they were all the same. Momma and Mimi had their chance at love and only gave it one. If either of them tried again, they could've found it. I'd admit that much.

Janelle pulled up in front of my building and parked on the street. "I hear you. Give me time. I'm not in a position to let anyone in the way you think I should. You had legit points, okay."

She exhaled. "Well, I guess that's more than before. You'd usually ignore my side altogether. I'll take that."

"Good. I'll see you later. Love you."

"Love you too. See how good it feels to say that and mean it? You could do that with a great guy."

"Girl, bye!" I got out and closed the door. She waited until I entered the building and drove off.

# SEVENTEEN

# Gianna

INSIDE MY APARTMENT, I SHOWERED AND PLOPPED ON the couch with a bottle of water. When I checked my phone, Zak had sent two more songs. "On My Way" by Tank was first. That came ten minutes ago. The other song, "No Conversation" by The Colleagues, did shit to me. Shit I didn't like.

The singer's tone was one thing. The lyrics and delivery were another. Zak did that on purpose. Every time the hook came, I closed my eyes and saw him hovering over me, bare-chested, lost inside me. I felt it right in the middle of my leaking love tunnel. The strokes in my thoughts were slow, hitting with every note.

I hopped to my feet. "Oh, hell naw, Gia! Get that crap out of your mind." Making my way to the kitchen for something to munch on, that tingle between my legs shot through me at each flash of Zak's face. "Nope! No, no, and fuck no!"

Wait! Was he on his way like the song? Why would he? *Gia, stop!*

The curiosity pushed my heart rate up. The only way to calm it was to find answers. I could call him to ask a stupid question. I'd ask who the hell he'd meant to send that song to. Or how many of his hoes did he send it to and did he think it'd be that easy with me?

Yeah, I'd go with that question. It sounded more like me. More like it didn't get to me.

After hitting his number in my contacts, each ring felt like horror film music. The kind leading to something I rarely wanted to see, but couldn't stop myself from looking. The anticipation fizzled when he didn't answer. Good. He was probably at home asleep. It was almost one in the morning. He wouldn't pop up at nobody's house that late.

The bed hadn't called my name yet, so Netflix it was. I got into a show called *The 100*. Willowridge's own, Isaiah Washington, starred in it. He never disappointed. Ever. Even as an ignorant bully toward Natalie Cole and Laurence Fishburne's characters in *Always Outnumbered, Always Outgunned*. Mimi had loved Laurence Fishburne.

I barely got through one episode when a knock at the door scared the shit out of me. *Who the hell?* It had to be someone with the wrong unit number. I rushed to the door and looked through the peephole.

Zakari. How the hell did he even get up here?

I eased off my tiptoes, resting my forehead against the door as he knocked another round. "Okay!" I opened it halfway. "What are you doing here?" No answer, only a leer that made me uncomfortably horny. I sucked my teeth. "I'm not one of your hoes. Come back at decent hours."

Zak rolled his eyes. "Don't start with that shit, Gia. You get my texts?"

"Yes."

"Why you ain't say nothing?"

"Why would I?"

He smacked his lips. "Man, you keep playing with me." He stepped closer to me and entered when I backed away.

"Nothing of the sort, Zaky." I crossed my arms over my chest.

"Stop that shit, Gia. I told you what that was."

"You told me what you want me to believe. Good thing I'm not stupid."

"Sure about that?"

"Um, you can get out."

"Why you so damn hard? How many ways can I show you?" He exhaled. "I want you. If I believed for a second you didn't feel the same about me, I wouldn't be doing all this shit."

"Nope, you'd be on top of Myesha." I rolled my eyes.

Zakari lowered his head, clenching his jaw. The fact her name bothered him may have meant he was telling the truth about her. Or he didn't like being called out on his bullshit. The latter sounded about right.

"What is it gonna take?" His head rose and eyes fell on mine.

I shrugged. "Why do you want me so bad? You can and probably get every woman you want."

"None of them girls come close to you. Not a damn one. I never wanted anyone like this."

"Zak, I can't do this with you."

"Why not?" he whined.

"Because you may really hurt me. After tonight with ol' girl, I realized some type of feelings developed because I wanted to fuck you up. I didn't like that feeling. You could do damage. I'd be dumb enough to let you in because of who you are. The way I might want you will take this to a place I don't want to go."

"I won't hurt you."

"Today said different."

"If I had you, nothing and no one else would come between us. The only damage I wanna do is in them guts." He closed the distance between us.

"Boy, shut yo' ass up." I took a few steps back and bumped into a bar stool. I turned to sit on it.

"For real. All the flirting and shit you did tonight ain't cool, G."

"Nigga, I don't belong to you."

"You will." A spark flowed through me with his confidence in those two words.

"Never. Stop sending me freaky songs. Save that for your—"

"You better not say that shit." He took a step closer, pointing at me.

I laughed at his finger in my face. "Fine. I'll mention one hoe. Myesha. She won't appreciate learning her Zaky sends freaky songs to other women."

"Gia, I promise you that wasn't a damn thing. She was to me what them other niggas were to you. You get it, right?"

"I do and like I said, I don't want to be on your roster." Zak didn't let me off the hook this time. He poked his lips out to the side. "Don't look at me like that. Even if the guys I messed with had others, I didn't know any of them personally. You are different."

"In a good way, I hope."

"In a dangerous way. You could really hurt me, Zakari. I don't want that kind of shit between us."

"Please believe if I had you, you'd be all I need. No roster, rotation, or whatever the hell else you wanna call it. Just you, Gia."

"You're not my type."

"So I guess Trevor's corny ass is." He rolled his eyes and

exhaled. "Or even Josh." Saying his name brought disgust to his face.

"Jealousy doesn't look good on you."

"Ain't nobody jealous. You'd have to be mine first and your scary ass can't handle that."

"Scary? First, I will never belong to no man. Get that straight. Second, I'm not trying to go there with you, Zak."

"You'd rather open an app for random dudes with all kinds of diseases or mental health issues that might get you sick or killed?"

"Why does it have to be the extreme with you? Maybe these guys are simply in the same boat. They want a good time with someone they don't have to interact with afterward."

"Yeah, until they catch feelings from the first hit and start stalking your ass like ol' boy."

"That is not what happened. That was all a coincidence."

"Bullshit! He could've drugged you and put you in a dungeon or some shit."

"Boy, you watch too much damn TV."

"You get what I mean. I ain't knocking your style. If you want to keep risking your life, that's on you."

"Rather that than my heart."

"With me, your heart wouldn't be at risk. I can guarantee that."

"Yeah, yeah, little boy. You're all talk."

"Ain't nothing little about me. You need to stop saying that shit before I have to show yo' ass."

A ping shot through me. Pantyliner be damned. Zak put me under a spell when his tongue swiped his bottom lip purposely slow.

I shook my head and dropped my eyes to the floor. "I don't want to see nothing you got."

"Oh, you don't, huh?" Zak moved my way, but I hurried and got up.

He laughed. "Why you runnin'?"

"I'm not." I leaned on the back of the couch. He met me there, resting on it right next to me. He pulled his shirt over his head. When it dropped to the floor, I stared at the wall across the room to avoid looking at him. "You need to put that back on."

"Nah. It's too hot in here. You need to get your AC checked."

It was hot but not from no damn thermostat. "What are you doing?"

"I told you, I'm hot."

"You think taking your..." Dammit, I looked. I might need to turn a fan on. His pecs were chiseled to perfection with abs that I wanted to touch, rub, lick—he had to go.

Zak smirked when I swallowed hard. In another minute, I wouldn't care who he was. This mini drought might benefit him if he didn't stop.

"Is there a problem? You seem a bit flustered at my little-boy body." He flexed his chest.

"You ain't funny, little boy."

Zak nodded his head with his lips pushed out. "You remember the last time I was here you wanted to see it."

When he pushed his thumbs on the inside of his boxer's waistband, I screeched. "No! You better not."

He bent over, laughing at my panic. It was so loud that I caught the giggles myself. Until I saw the outline through his jeans. Shit!

"Get your behind out of here, Zakari."

He snorted. "Let me see something first." He pulled his

phone from his pocket and scrolled around. I kept my seat next to him, acting like a shy schoolgirl next to a confident jock. Not knowing if I should walk away or wait.

A song started. The "No Conversation" song. Dammit, Zakari!

Zak's mouth moved and a voice I'd never heard came out. He sang along. Lower than the artist, but sounded good. Too good. He bent his index finger and nicked the bottom of my chin. Pulling me in front of him with no contest, he had me. My love canal throbbed in eagerness to feel him. Logic mattered no more.

By the time he got to the chorus, my mouth crashed into his. The man's hands wrapped around me. One on my ass and the other right above it. He squeezed with the right amount of force to express his need for me at that moment. The connection between our lips and our tongues fighting to taste the other took me to another place. He broke away.

Zak waited until my eyes opened. All I saw were his moistened lips, then our eyes met. "I want you," he whispered.

"I want you too." My breaths were short and heavy once I'd resumed breathing.

"You mean it? I don't want you regretting it in the morning."

"It's already morning. Now stop talking." I stared at his lips again before tugging the bottom one with my teeth.

He smirked once I let it go. "I thought you didn't kiss."

"I don't."

He pressed his mouth onto mine, exhaling through his nostrils. We walked backward once he stood up and took steps forward. Zak's hands grabbed onto my waist and lifted me onto my kitchen island.

"Take your clothes off." His breathy demand caused no

hesitation. I did what he said, pulling my oversized tee over my head, revealing my bare breasts.

Zak spread my knees apart, getting between them. His eyes never left my breasts. When he touched them, my eyes shut. His hands were warm and moist from sweat, I assumed. Meaning he was as nervous as I was before this moment.

Those long, thick fingers rubbed against my right nipple. When my attention traveled to Zak's face, he gazed at my breasts like he was trying to become acquainted with them. "You're more beautiful than I dreamed you'd be." It brought a smile across my face.

That smile soon puckered for him, getting closer to my lips, connecting to me as if this was our normalcy. His hand went to the back of my head as he pressed harder against my mouth. Our tongues couldn't get any closer, yet I wanted them to. I scooted to the edge of the island, pulling him further between my thighs.

His chest heaved, pressing onto my breasts with every inhale. I found his belt and unbuckled it before pulling that sucker through the loops and tossing it on the floor. Then I went for the button of his jeans to remove the layers of clothes between us. I saw the tip of his dick peek through his boxers.

I bit my lip at the thought of what that thing would feel like. A little more than what I'd experienced. I would take all of it. Or at least try to.

Zak's brow raised at my exhale. He knew what he had and how above-average his shit was. No wonder he had a lot of women. They'd wanted to get a piece of this no matter the circumstance.

His lips feathered mine once more before they kissed down to my neck to my breasts. His mouth covered the left one while he thumbed the right. My head dropped back at his warm tongue, lapping my areola.

Zakari Jarell Lawrence could do the type of damage that'd have me feeling like it was worth it. I ain't even have his dick yet and all my fight, even mentally, left me.

*What the fuck, Gia?*

# EIGHTEEN

# Zakari

THE TASTE OF GIA'S SKIN HAD MY DICK IN PAIN, yearning to feel her wrapped around it. I was in no rush, though. She'd meet the motherfucking beast in due time.

Her nipples were some shades darker than her already gorgeous rich walnut exterior. I nibbled on each one before licking my way to her navel. I gently bit her stomach, only to feel her jerk a bit. Gia hit my arm and laughed. "Don't be biting me!" Smart-ass always had something to say. "Let's go to my room." She tried to get down from the island.

"Nah, I got you." I gripped both ass cheeks and slid her all the way to me.

When I lifted her, she held on tightly. "You better not drop me, Zakari."

"Be quiet. You ain't runnin' nothin'. Where's the room?"

"Straight back." We passed three doors until we got to her bedroom. As soon as I got close enough, I threw her on the bed. She shrieked, thinking she'd land on the floor. I wouldn't do that to her. Not on purpose, at least.

"Punk ass." She couldn't stop laughing at herself.

Gia was in rare form. Willing. She was a hard-ass with

everything for as long as I'd known her. Seeing her open up to me had a nigga wanting more than what I was about to do to her.

I got on my knees on the bed as she laid back. After slowly peeling her panties off, I stared at her bare body beneath me in awe. This was fucking Gia Jameson. I couldn't get my thoughts straight. I wanted every part of her and had to decide what I'd devour first.

I spread her legs, pulling her closer before resting on my stomach. Her love rested centimeters away from my face. This shit differed from any other time I'd faced a woman this way. In the pit of my stomach, I knew she would be the absolute last one.

Brushing my nose across her labia, she shuddered. I licked one side and bit her lip as she moaned in anticipation. I finally covered her with my mouth, salivating.

Her essence covered my tongue. Gia's movement proved I did what she liked. I sucked on the hole I'd enter with my aching dick soon, taking in all that she put out.

For minutes, I tongue fucked her while thumbing her clit. I wanted her to come more than once. It didn't take long before her dam broke all over my tongue. I licked every drop.

When her back arched, Gia appeared spent. Too bad. I flickered her clit with the tip of my tongue as she yelped. I wouldn't let her off that easily.

Tasting Gia meant tasting all of her. Licking every part of her, nibbling, biting, tugging on her sensitive nub. I remembered her calling it a bean. I devoured that motherfucker like it was the protein I needed to live. Her bean was her weakness. She came two more times, screaming louder and louder.

"Zak! Fuck!" she squealed during her latest quake. She

tried pulling herself away from my mouth, but I didn't let her. She was going to take everything this little boy did to her. Her punishment for that smart ass, sexy ass mouth.

I kissed her inner thighs, making my way to her belly button. Her breasts needed attention, so I gave it to them, biting them along the way. When I reached her face, her eyes shut as she took my bottom lip into her mouth, savoring herself. That shit made me even harder.

Gia lifted her head to get closer to my mouth, shoving her tongue in it. With authority, she sucked on my tongue, getting every bit of her flavor from me. I could knock her up right now for that shit.

"You got a condom?" she whispered.

"Yeah. Hold up."

The cool air emphasized the absence of her heat. I quickly found my jeans on the floor near the kitchen, removing the gold package from my wallet. I reentered her bedroom, ready to go. Gia posted up on her elbows, examining my dick with her gaze. "Don't just shove it in. That thing looks..." She laughed. "I sound like a punk right now."

"Nah, you sound concerned that this little boy ain't as little as you thought." I covered the body part she stared at with a thin layer of protection.

Gia laughed louder. "Zakari, I cannot believe we're doing this."

I got on the bed and hovered over her. "Believe that shit. Ain't no turning back now."

"I'm not trying to. It just seems...mmm." I brushed the tip against her dripping wet opening.

"You better not hurt me."

"I'm too little for all that."

A smile spread across her face. "Like you said, ain't

nothing little about you." I smirked at her, finally admitting she was wrong in so many words.

Gia laid back as I spread her legs even further. I rubbed my dick against her clit until her back arched in the position I needed her in. I pushed inside her, dropping my head at the instant pool covering me. "Damn, Gia."

She was tighter than I thought she'd be. I took a deep breath and inched my way inside, trying not to think about how fucking good it felt. The shit hit different with her. I'd been inside some bomb pussy, but Gia's was getting to me at the first touch.

Her moans and faint shrieks didn't help. Her face twisted the deeper I got until she put her hands on my chest to stop me from going further. I pulled out and pushed in a little further, with her releasing another scream of pleasure and pain.

"Zak, I can't."

"Yes you can, baby. Relax."

She shifted herself beneath me, taking deep, slow breaths.

"Gia, look at me." She did. "I will never hurt you. You know that, right?" She nodded.

I covered her mouth with mine. While tongue fighting, I pushed my dick all the way in. It slid straight in from the help of her being so wet, but she screamed into my mouth. I ignored her punch to my chest because her eyes rolled to the back of her head as she moaned.

"Damn, Zak. Yes, baby. Yes!" she whispered. She'd have to stop saying shit like that when I was trying to keep from nutting too fast.

With every stroke, she winced but took it. I kept the pace slow for her to get used to me. Once her shoulders released all the tension, I knew she was ready for me to do what I came to do.

I lifted a bit and raised her thigh to get in some more. Gia screamed and grabbed one of my hands, squeezing it with each flash of pain. I could tell from her face. I didn't want to hurt her.

"You need me to stop?"

"Fuck no. Just...keep going. I can...oh, shit. Mmm." Her body stiffened as the pressure of her orgasm clenched around my dick. "Fuck, Zakari."

Gia fucking changed me with that. I saw her love faces, heard her moans, her screams. Her pussy contracted around my dick like it was meant to. She fucking owned me and we hadn't even finished.

Gia coming apart from my touch fucked me up. I sped up with harder strokes, watching her breasts bounce around in circles. Gia never quieted down. All her sounds egged me on until my nuts tightened. It was too soon, but it was already happening.

Without warning, I held her hips and plunged into her over and over. Gia hollered and cussed me out with every thrust. Less than a minute later, those thrusts slowed down as my seeds filled the tip of the condom. Watching those eyes roll back again with her thighs gripping my waist was the icing on the cake. Cake I got to have, eat, and fuck.

When her orgasm ended, I slowly pulled out. I went to the bathroom to flush the condom. "Where are your towels?"

"In the...cabinet behind...the door."

I smiled at the reason she could barely say shit. I finally had Gia. Ain't no going back from that shit. No one ever came close to her.

I held a towel under hot water and cleaned myself off. I got another towel, ran it under the water, and squeezed out the excess. I handed it to Gia, who was half asleep.

"Thank you," was all she got out. She took the towel and cleaned herself.

"I guess I should leave now."

One of her eyes popped open as she sat up slowly. I reached out for the towel. "If you don't get yo' ass in this bed."

I chuckled at how she could still talk to me crazy. "I thought you didn't let niggas stay afterward."

"I guess you're not just any nigga then."

My heart damn near stopped after hearing that from her hardheaded ass. Her naked body laid there, all worn out, and that was only the first time. We took it easy tonight.

"Besides, somebody will have to help me out of bed when I wake up. You broke my shit. I can barely feel my damn legs." She laughed weakly.

I did what she told me and got in the bed. "You crazy. You know that?"

Gia turned around to face me, still with only one eye open. "You are officially no longer a little boy in my book." She pushed me but didn't move me. It was a weak attempt. Her smirk quickly left as she dropped her head onto her pillow. "You knocked my ass out."

"Good. That's what you get for talking all that shit."

"I'ma kick yo' ass if I can't walk tomorrow."

I laughed at her threats even while she was half asleep. I watched her doze off and got away with trailing my finger on her shoulder down to her hand. Her disheveled hair made my dick twitch since I was the one who did that to her.

Gia slept peacefully. I kissed her forehead, then her nose, and finally closed my eyes. All I could see were the many faces that were now ingrained in my brain. No way would I fuck this up. Gia was mine.

# NINETEEN

# Gianna

I opened my eyes to his crooked mouth resting on my pillow. I watched him sleep peacefully while his heavy arm kept me in place. My thigh topped his, entangled too much to break away without waking him.

Dammit, I swore this wouldn't happen. Now, I never wanted to go without it.

The tingle in my middle in a non-sexual way forced me to disturb his sleep. The bathroom called me. Zak only turned the other way.

While I was in the shower, the bathroom door creaked open. "Boy, get out!"

"I gotta pee."

"Go to the other bathroom, Zak."

"Why? It ain't like I'm not acquainted with your naked body. I'll be quick."

"No. That's nasty. Get out." I thought he had left until I heard his stream slightly over the shower head. "Ugh, you don't fucking listen."

The man was as hardheaded as me. We'd never work in

any other capacity than what we established last night. I soaked my face towel until it had a streaming drip.

I held one corner of the towel and flung it over the shower door a few times before he flushed the toilet. I didn't release the towel since the excess water did the job I aimed for.

Zak sucked his teeth. "Ahh, man! You play too damn much," Zak yelled.

After he washed his hands, he searched through my drawers for something. Seconds later, it became apparent he'd found my stash of new toothbrushes.

"There's a guest bathroom for a reason."

"Shut up," he barely got out as he brushed his teeth.

I carried on with my shower. The water hit my skin the way I needed. Peace returned the second he left the bathroom.

When I faced the shower door, it swung open, bringing a bit of a breeze with it. "What are you doing?" I looked at his hand. The steam made it hard, so I leaned forward. "Motherfucker, you'd better not."

Zakari held a bottle of baby oil. "You started it."

"Zakari, do not play."

"Next time you better watch how you talk to me."

"Okay, damn!"

"Say you sorry."

"Ugh, I'm sorry. Please don't."

Zak closed the shower door. He got on my damn nerves. Why did his package have to come with the rest of him? His dumb ass had me on edge. I didn't trust him.

I closed my eyes for one last wash. This was at least my third round. Parts of the water got cold on my back, then I smelled baby oil the same moment I slipped. "You motherfucker!" He pulled his hand back from the top of the door.

My shower was small enough to hold myself up between the wall and glass door. I had like five close calls before I finally stepped out onto the rug.

Zakari's howls echoed, causing me to laugh too. After drying myself, I took one step toward him, but slid the entire way to the sink. "You stupid son of a bitch! You put it on the floor too?" I swung at him but missed as he flew out the door.

My ribs hurt from all the laughing. He'd started a damn war with that move. "You better sleep with one eye open." I dropped my towel on the floor, covering the oil. I carefully made it to my bedroom. "I swear you will regret that."

"Shit, the only thing I regret is not recording your face."

"I hate you." Zak snatched my naked body over to him. I elbowed him in the gut. "Hell, naw. You ain't touching me after pulling that. It's on."

***

I UNLOCKED THE PADLOCK TO THE STORAGE WITH MY mom and Mimi's things. Our photo albums had to be somewhere in this room. Blair must've gotten the largest unit in this place.

After moving a few boxes, I found one labeled "Momma's books" and got excited. She mainly had Brenda Jackson, Zane, and Eric Jerome Dickey books. I'd read them all.

Small notebooks covered the bottom of the box. I fanned through one, discovering Momma's handwriting on every page. It immediately jump-started my heart. They were her journals.

Momma used to write in these almost nightly. When I should've been asleep, she'd be on her side of the bed writing away. I remember wondering what she wrote about, but never with enough curiosity to crack them open before now. There had to be at least ten journals in this box. I put it to the side to take home.

Another ten minutes passed before I located two other boxes with photo albums and picture frames. I had expected this Saturday to be only about me reminiscing with the photos. Momma's journals made it more interesting.

I locked up and packed the few boxes into my car. Zak called me on the way home, trying to come over. It'd be the third time this week.

"Whatchu doing later today?" he asked.

"Not you, nigga! You acting a little sprung already."

He chuckled through my speakers. "Nah, I was only tryna chill."

"Let me guess, watch Netflix, too?"

"We can. I'll pick up some Lotus."

"Man, you shoulda led with that."

"Greedy ass."

"You should have plenty of pizza still, though." I laughed but he didn't. Two days ago, I ordered seven pizzas to his house for him to pay for in cash. Each had a letter in pepperoni. All together, they spelled baby oil.

"Man, they lucky I had cash on me. That's fucked up. I had to pass pizzas out to my neighbors like a dumb ass because of you. I told them a girl who's tryna get with me sent them."

"They believed you?"

"Hey, it was free food."

"I guess. Anyway, I'll text you my order. What time?"

"Later tonight. I just finished playing golf with my dad. We 'bout to have lunch at my parents' house after I stop home for a shower."

"That'll work."

"Bet. Later."

I stopped by Salata for a salad so I'd have an appetite later. I ate my food as I roamed through Mimi's first box. Her dated frames held the pictures so long they peeled and stuck to the glass after attempting to remove them.

The second box was easier to sort through. Mimi always made me and Momma pose for impromptu pictures with the disposable cameras she kept on her at all times. I found a few Sears photos too. I finally had everything I needed to display my two favorite women around my place.

A whole hour disappeared from my lingered stares at these memories. Janelle would trip at the ones of her. Those buck teeth were a faint memory until now. She grew into them in high school, but these were classic embarrassing photos. I smiled and laughed at each one I remembered.

I pulled the last box over to my bookcase to add Momma's books to my collection. The journals got my attention last. I grabbed three of them and snuggled in my favorite spot on the couch, ready to get into my mom's mind. I didn't expect much except prayers. She used to always tell me to write my prayers in a journal. I assumed that was what she did most of the time.

The first couple of entries proved me right. Momma thanked God for getting her new apartment. I had to be about three years old when she had started this one. I teared up as I rubbed the penmanship on the paper. These were really my mom's books. She had touched these and poured herself into them. I hugged the book as if it was her.

"God, I miss you, Ma."

I skipped to the middle of the book. She wrote about being so grateful for finding the Cabbage Patch Doll I begged her for. Apparently, it was my fourth birthday gift. She didn't know how she'd get one. Wow.

I skimmed through the next few until something caught my eye.

*1/25/1999*

*Dear diary,*

*It's been a while. I've been so busy with work, Gia, and Momma. Nothing major happened lately. Well, not until today. I saw him. He looked so good. I hate how much I wanted to touch him. Blair still had my heart. I don't want it that way. It hurts to know how much I hurt him. Momma needed me more than he did. Now, I realize I needed him too. Gia could have had it all if only I went with him. We talked about what could have been. I hated it all. He's married, but I still wished we could do more than talk. Lord, forgive me.*

*Blair ruined it when he demanded to see Gia. Demanded. Can you believe that? I hadn't seen him in five years. All he cared about was seeing Gia. She didn't know him. Had never met him. Momma doesn't know I sent him pictures of Gia. After he wrote to me so much while in school, I couldn't help but feel bad for not going with him. He wasn't happy with that woman. He kept telling me he'd leave it all if I told him to. I could never do that. Momma would have a whole fit and a half if I went against her wishes. She was only looking out for me. I love her so much. She gave me life and sacrificed a ton for me to be where I am today. She helps me with Gia every day. I think she does it more for herself. We haven't been the same since I moved out. I only did it because I wanted my own space.*

*I dated this sweet guy, but it went nowhere because I could never bring him home. Momma was always there. He couldn't wait for me. Typical. Seeing Blair today reminded me of how lonely I am. Lord, if true love is real, I would like to have it. I'm hoping that Blair was not the only man I could love.*

*4/16/1999*
*Dear Diary,*

*Blair wrote me a letter today. His wife had his daughter last month. Can you tell me why I cried as I read those words? He moved on with his life as he should. I let Momma keep me here when all I wanted to do was go with him. He wants Gia and this new baby to grow up in each other's lives. He asked to be present in her life. Blair has my address. Sometimes I wished he would just come for us. If he still loved me the way he always says he does, why can't he come on his own? He asks and I say no. But I really want him to. My answer used to be because of Momma's warnings. Really, I don't want to see him if I can't be with him. Gia might hate me for being so selfish when she's old enough to understand. But having him around as only her father wasn't enough for me. Lord, how can I stop feeling this way?*

I slammed the book shut. None of this even sounded like my mother. It was her handwriting, but how could she have felt that way?

"Shit." I rested my head back on the couch. He was telling the truth.

Damn, I felt like an asshole.

Momma lied. The story was always the same my entire life. Blair left us and immediately married someone else. Momma made it sound like he thought she wasn't good enough for him. The throbbing in my head traveled to my belly.

I didn't know what angered me more. A great deal of Blair's absence being my mother's doing or that I'd have to go to him and apologize. His texts and calls all this time had gone unanswered.

After cutting all communication, I'd tried to pay my rent. I didn't want Blair paying for anything for me. The account had no balance. He still paid it after I went in and changed the bank information to my account.

Blair's guilt came in the form of taking care of me financially. Even though I didn't need it, he took it upon himself. My guilt seeped in after realizing all that he'd done in the recent past and how ungrateful I may have seemed. The man asked to see me frequently. Each request went ignored. Luckily, he still didn't pop up on people like my mother wanted him to do back then.

How many entries were like this? Shit, the answer to that was not a desire of mine. I'd seen enough for now.

Dammit, Momma.

# TWENTY

# Zakari

At dinner with my family, Janelle kept narrowing her eyes at me. Gia didn't tell her about us since she acted paranoid as hell whenever we were together. We stayed out of the streets so we wouldn't run into anyone. Either her place or mine.

The way my sister acted, I pulled her to the side before dessert. "Fuck wrong witchu? Why you looking at me like that?"

"Nigga, 'cause you glowing like you carrying life or something." She amused herself with that one.

"You childish."

There she went, squinting them big ass eyes again. "So, is it the girl from Main Event? Mya. No, Misha. Keisha?"

"Her name doesn't matter because that shit was over and done before you met her."

"She was all 'Zaky and I are in love.' How is it over already?"

"Yo, something is wrong with her. It was never anything serious or close to even giving her that impression."

"Hmm, I thought that's what got into you that night.

You've been different ever since. It couldn't be Gia after what she said about you and your little kiss."

"What kiss?" Or rather, which one? Saying too much too soon would give away more than I needed. Nelle had to say the words first.

"Something about you kissing her. That was a while ago and by the way you acted that night, you turned her off. Although, I think she's messing with somebody, too. Maybe Trevor. Cameron hadn't mentioned anything, though."

"That cornball. What cubicle that nigga came out of?"

"Why you pressed? Looks like you're preoccupied, anyway. When will we meet her? I'm sure Mom will be happy to learn you have the capability of being more than a hoe."

"What did you say?" Mom snuck up on us. "You in here calling each other hoes?" She snickered.

"That's your bad-mouth daughter. I would never call her anything but a nosy angel," I told my mom, hugging her from the side.

Dad called us to the living room, claiming he'd eat dessert without us. My dad's sweet tooth waited for no man. We joined him after grabbing our plates of apple pie.

Janelle promised she wouldn't toss me to the wolves this dinner. In return, I'd have to double date with her and Cameron with my assumed girl to keep her quiet. Gia wouldn't go for that, so my time ticked down until Janelle put my parents on my trail. Hopefully, it wouldn't grow cold, and I'd have proof that a woman was constantly occupying my thoughts.

Gia canceled on me the other night. She said she wasn't feeling well and wouldn't let me come over to check on her. I figured she wanted to be alone.

We've been kicking it for almost a month and the shit frustrated the fuck out of me. I ain't had nobody to blame but myself.

Before, Gianna Renae Jameson was a young boy's fantasy. I'd most likely find a bomb-ass woman to take the place of a childish imagination. Story over. But I touched the forbidden fruit. Smelled it, tasted it, felt it on the inside.

That woman had me all in my head. I wanted more than she'd give. I also didn't want our thing to end. Settling down was further along my timeline; however, I'd do it this second for Gia.

My dad and I got back from the shooting range. Mom went out of town to visit my aunt, which meant I'd spend much time with my pops.

Byron came half an hour after us. He picked up some saltfish and ackee, Jamaican patties, and curry chicken and roti. His uncle was from Trinidad and had a restaurant on his side of town. I'd been waiting all day for this food.

"Now, that's good right there." Dad wiped his mouth. "Y'all want a beer?" he asked, heading to the kitchen.

"Yes, sir," Byron said.

"Me, too."

"When I get back, you can tell me more about this young lady your sister said you're hiding from us."

My head popped up right when Byron's eyes landed my way. "Your Pops knows about Gia?"

I shook my head. "No one does."

"So, who's the lucky lady?" My dad handed us each a beer bottle.

"Your daughter talks too much about stuff she knows

nothing of. I'm not with nobody, Pops. Otherwise, I might end up like this one." I nudged Byron. "I'm surprised to see him out so much. He's been hiding up under his lady for so long."

"Shit, that's the best place to be when it's good." Pops dipped his chin at Byron.

"I've been telling your son! He keeps messing with all these women instead of finding one to kick it with."

"Well, that's a one-sided conversation with this boy." Dad elbowed me. "He gets a whiff of free cookies and goes crazy. That'll get old fast but he gotta learn on his own."

"Y'all see me sitting here, right? I do what I does because I can and I want to. When the time comes for me to do otherwise, I will. In the meantime, let me do me."

"My dude, you letting too many women do you. You gon' end up in a situation you can't get out of if you don't be careful."

"B, I'm careful. Damn! I know what I'm doing."

"He's getting riled up. Let's leave him alone about it. He will learn or get lucky." Dad still talked to Byron like I wasn't sitting in the middle of them.

I finally got them off my case as we checked out Yasuke. We couldn't let a Black Samurai anime hit Netflix and not support it.

As soon as I got up to throw my trash away, a soft knock at the door stole our attention. Few people had my address. Nelle usually banged on the door like the police every time she came over. It cracked her up.

I checked the peephole. Whoever was out there wasn't clearly in view. "Who is it?"

"Zak, is that you?" a woman asked. There was only one woman with that voice, yet I couldn't figure out how the hell she found my apartment.

I tried to change my voice. "Nah, you got the wrong place."

"Zaky, that's you in there. Stop joking."

Byron walked over to me, asking who it was. I whispered her name. "Myesha."

"Come on, dawg. You still messing with that girl?"

"No. She never came to my house either. So, put two and two together. Girlie is crazy."

Byron nodded, as if he had a plan. He hit my chest and waved for me to get out of sight. I took the hint and waited in the hall.

The door opened. "Uh, hi. I'm not sure who you're looking for, but it's not me," Byron told her.

"Oh, I'm sorry. I thought for sure I watched him go in this...wait a minute. You were with Zak at Main Event. So, either you're lying or you are roommates. I'm sure he came here."

"Lady, you're mistaken. Be safe out there knocking on random doors looking for whoever you're looking for."

"When you're done lying for your boy, you tell him I have important news regarding our child."

Dad's eyes darted at me. I rushed to the door, pulling it all the way open. "What the hell are you talking about?"

"I do have the right place."

Byron returned to his seat to what would surely be a show. The woman had a thing for building up our relationship in her head.

"Yo, for real, Myesha. How did you even find me? You been following me?"

"A girl's gotta do what she gotta do."

"Man, this is crazy. I told you to stop with all this shit. What are you even doing?"

"I needed to tell you something. You won't give me a

chance to talk on the phone and it's nothing I can tell you in a text." She crossed her arms over her cleavage. Her hip poked out further as she took a stance.

"Knowing yo' ass will lie to get attention. Let's hear it. I'll bite."

"Not in front of company. We can do that later." She bit her bottom lip and winked.

"Myesha, what do you need to tell me?"

"Oh!" She opened her purse and handed me a glossy piece of paper. "That's our baby."

I stumbled backward until the door caught me. Dad rose to his feet. "What's going on here?"

"Hello, sir. Everything is okay. I was only telling Zakari we are having a baby."

I glued my attention to the sonogram in my hands. "I strapped up," I whispered. At least I thought I had.

"Well, when it's meant to be, even a condom can't stop destiny," she said with too much excitement. The smile on her face turned my stomach.

"Son, is this true?"

"You're his dad? Oh, my gosh! It's so nice to meet you. I'm Myesha. I'm sure we'll see more of each other from now on. Zaky is such an amazing boyfriend."

Byron tapped my chest twice with the back of his hand. "You a'ight, man?"

I shook my head, keeping my eyes on the black-and-white picture between my fingers. My next thought flew to Gia.

Pregnant? Myesha? My brain throbbed like someone had hit me with a skillet or some shit. I retreated to my bathroom for a second of peace. A million thoughts ran through my mind as I splashed cold water on my face. I rushed out once I realized something.

All three of them were sitting in the living room. "How you so sure this is my baby?"

"Son?!"

"Hold up, Pops. She has a kid with her man already. It's most likely his. How you figure it's mine?"

"Because you're the only one I've been with in months, Zaky."

"Bullshit!" I yelled, because I wanted my conclusion to be right more than anything. She'd have to prove it with a paternity test first.

"Calm down, Zak," Byron suggested.

I'd seen her play games before. Her acting fooled many, but not me. "Myesha, I don't mean no disrespect, but come back to me when the kid is born. I'll get my own DNA test done to find out if what you're saying is true. Until then, I don't want to see you."

Myesha stood to her feet with a quickness. "What?! Why? You messing with that Gia bitch. Is that why you won't talk to me? I'm the mother of your child!"

"No the fuck you ain't. Not until a test confirms that shit, it ain't true. Keep Gia's name outcho mouth."

"Gia, Gia, Gia. Now what? We'll see what miss thing thinks about your child growing in me."

"You better stay the fuck away from her." I stepped to her. Although I wouldn't put my hands on her, it was enough for my father to get between us.

"Young lady, I'm gonna have to ask you to leave," he said.

"Gladly. You will see me again." Myesha stomped out of my apartment and slammed the door behind her.

"Fuck, man!" I kicked over the table that held our food and drinks.

My dad approached me, placing his hands on each side

of my shoulders. "You need to relax, son. If what she says is true, I raised you to be responsible. That won't be a question. Right now, you need to focus on you and the choices you've made that got you here." He released me.

"I know. I know. But pregnant? I didn't get that girl pregnant, Pops. She gotta be lying." At that moment, the possibility of her telling the truth gut-punched me again. I bit my bottom lip to stop it from trembling. I shook my head over and over. "No, no, no. Hell, naw. This ain't happening to me right now. Tell me this ain't happening." I paced the dining area near my table.

Byron had already cleaned up most of the mess I made. He didn't say a word.

I wasn't ready to be a dad, but Gia was who'd I'd rather get this news from. Not no damn Myesha.

I found myself in the bathroom again, facing the mirror. "What the fuck did you do?"

# TWENTY-ONE

# Gianna

I picked up my phone to call Blair, but my fingers would not cooperate. For weeks, he'd sent texts to check on me. I still hadn't gained the guts to tell him I knew the truth.

Unfortunately, learning my mother had lied to me meant acknowledging Blair hadn't. Admitting it proved to be more challenging than consuming all of this new information.

Momma wrote so many damn details about her life and feelings throughout. I damn near rewatched my whole life in a different lens. My parents had loved each other. For real, loved each other. All this time, she'd fed me the exact opposite story.

Then there were the other men Momma dated. I had no clue about not one of them. She didn't mention love in those entries. However, this lady said a few guys put voodoo on her in the bed. I had to admit that part was funny and refreshing because I assumed my poor momma was a damn nun for a minute. All them nights at Mimi's was her time to get her grown woman on.

Part of reading over ten of her journals made me feel closer to her. It was so fucked up that Momma misled me with the storyline she forced me to believe about her and Blair. Whatever she'd said was the last word about it. I had no reason to question her. I regretted it.

I had ignored Shana and Blair's tag-teaming calls long enough. Olivia and Jonah didn't deserve me ghosting them. Because I actually loved those little people, I took a deep breath and hit the phone icon. I'd let it ring at least three times before hanging up.

Halfway through the first ring, Blair's voice came from the other end. "Hello. Gianna? Is that you?"

"Uh, yeah. Um...I was just returning your call. Well, calls."

Blair exhaled loudly through my speaker. I imagined a smile along with it. "I'm glad you called. We've missed you so much. I wanted to come over, but Shana said it wasn't a good idea. I was worried about you."

"I'm okay. I actually wanted to...um...talk, I guess. About my mom and things."

"Gia, we don't need to. I understand how hard things are and I'm sorry for everything I said the last time we were together. It wasn't right for me to—"

"No, I'm sorry, Blair. I blamed you for a lot of shit growing up. I mean, you weren't there, so I'm not apologizing for stuff I said about that. We can both say you weren't present, but it's more clear as to why. The reality possibly differed from what I was taught about you." I heard him snicker in the background. "What's so funny?"

"Nothing, sweetheart. I never envisioned this day would come. I was prepared to maintain my innocence forever. Well, as you mentioned, only partial innocence. I was painfully wrong for not trying hard enough to be a part of your life."

"Yes, you were. In hindsight, Momma's side of the story changed my view of you. I didn't like you, so I wouldn't have let you in. You still should've tried, though."

"You're right. I failed you back then. I will make it up to you until the day I die. Gia, I'm so glad to get to this place with you. Even in the recent years, I perceived you didn't fully forgive me. I had to accept it, but I'm hoping we can start anew now that everything is out."

"I'm open to a fresh start." A smile spread across my lips. "One thing, though. I can pay my own bills, Blair."

"You will. One day."

"Seriously. It's weird that you pay my rent. I have a career. I make good money."

"Okay. I will stop paying your rent when you get married. How about that?"

"So, now you got jokes."

"What are you in here laughing about?" Shana asked in the background.

Blair filled her in before putting her on speakerphone. "Gia! We missed you."

A peace fell on me now that I accepted that her love was genuine. I grinned and rolled my eyes. They were going to make this so cheesy. "I missed y'all too."

"It's so good to hear your voice. You know since you can't call nobody." Shana imitated Jerome and jacked it all up.

I burst out laughing. "Uh-uh, please don't. Leave that to Martin 'cause nah."

"Don't hate on my greatness." She giggled. "So, someone is having a birthday in a couple of weeks."

"I wouldn't miss Liv's party for anything. Even for your deadbeat dad of a husband."

"Whoa! Whoa! I'm still on the phone," Blair said.

"What? Too soon?" We cracked up even though I respected what he had at least tried to do since I'd lost my family.

"God, it is so good to hear you laugh again, Gia. I'm sorry for my part in hurting you, but I'm here now. I will always be here."

"I trust you will."

Momma did what she felt was best; even though it caused more damage than good, I still loved my mom. She gave me everything within her power. Blair punked out throughout my childhood but stepped it up so I'd take the win.

Sometimes, I wondered if his other two daughters would ever come around to him. His e-wife blocked their interaction after they divorced. Blair was with them financially until they became adults themselves. I've only seen pictures of them. Maybe one day he'll have all of his children in his life. I hoped their mom didn't pull an Elaine and fill their heads with lies too.

Although, I loved and respected my mother's teachings, I needed to unlearn some things. Trashing Blair was one. The constant pushback with Zak was another.

I hated the way my body reacted with every thought of him. Or the uptick in my heart's rhythm whenever I heard his voice. Men had no type of control over me. None. Around that man, I barely had control of myself.

We'd hang out with only chilling in mind. I'd talk to myself before Zak's arrival, pleading with my body to behave. The moment I lay eyes on him, I caved. I craved the feeling of him inside me more than anything. I'd gotten acquainted with all he was slanging.

Other times, it was more than the sex. Zakari Lawrence had a side of him I was so honored to have met. We laughed and joked, but he seriously had a soft side. He was heavy in his feelings about so many things in our world, from systematic oppression to global warming.

He donated time and money to organizations he believed in. As crazy as it sounded, this fool was active in his church. He mentored teens in his church's young entrepreneurs program.

As much as Zak played around, he was serious about his business and helping others be better at handling theirs. Black Owned Moguls was a program he founded with two other men a few years ago. They train up young Black people on how to build, run, and conduct business. One of his partners used to work as a stockbroker full-time. Now, he passes down his knowledge of investing with our community.

Zak was a part of something so incredible. I would've never guessed it from his behavior. I couldn't say much about the hoeish side because I had my own. However, his big goofy, play-too-damn-much ass had me fooled. I figured he'd be another number in someone else's business like most of us were.

We discussed what I'd be interested in if I started a business. I still wasn't sure, but Zak had planted a seed in my head on ownership one day. Zak had layers I'd enjoyed peeling back when we spent time together.

What we had surpassed mind-blowing sex. Zakari had become a genuine friend.

Could I call it friends with benefits? Maybe. Deep down, if I was honest, I wanted more. He was sweet, thoughtful, caring, giving, and so damn sexy. I couldn't think of him and not obsess on the pure sexiness God blessed him with.

When my monthly visitor came, Zak came over after work with junk food and Fireball. I'd talk his head off for hours and he's listen. We chilled and tried to get through a movie. Until my dumb ass tried to give him head. I couldn't ignore my urge to please him.

I hadn't done it in so long. I wished I had because Zak's blessed appendage was not the best way to break me in. My jaws hurt for days after getting only half of him in my mouth. He clowned me for it even though his ass came only a minute or two after my lips touched him.

Things between us were awkwardly good. I enjoyed spending time with him. Whether wrapped in his arms or my legs wrapped around him, Zak made me happy. It messed with my head and my heart.

All the shit I talked about not falling for anyone flew out the damn window once I opened up to him. Sometimes I contemplated on shutting it all down to save myself from the inevitable. Sometimes, I was curious about where it led. I wanted to find out for myself if what everyone else told me was true. Could I actually have something real with someone who wouldn't hurt me?

# TWENTY-TWO

# Zakari

I SWITCHED UP MY ROUTINE. MYESHA FINDING OUT where I lived meant she knew too much about my moves.

Gia didn't care that I asked if we only met at her place from now on. It was still safe. She accepted my excuse of not liking her driving home from my place at night.

I changed gyms in case that was where the stalking had started. Myesha might've told the truth about everything. Even she should see her approach was all fucked up. She appeared as some psycho-ass woman I wished I'd never met. As my grandmother would say, what's done is done.

Nelle's nosy ass sniffed around after she noticed my preoccupation. Work took the blame. Big sis wouldn't push since she couldn't do anything about it if it were true.

Gia got another round from me. The shit worked like therapy until it ended. When I was inside her, nothing else mattered. The outside world typically disappeared when we spent time together.

After what Myesha had dropped on me, sex was the only time I didn't obsess about my mess. As much as I wanted to talk to Gia about it, I couldn't.

With all the playing around and talk about this being nothing more than scratching her itch, Gia became someone I confided in. Over the last couple of months, she'd been a friend to me. I swore I'd keep in that lane to protect myself. The more we talked, the more I saw her. It made me comfortable enough to tell her shit about me. She'd slowly turned my ass into Byron and I didn't completely hate it.

I rested on my arm beside her in her bed. Gia surprised me when she let her guard down. We fit together more that she'd admit. We understood each other. Everything I wanted was within reach but unattainable at the same time.

Gia flicked my forehead and rolled her eyes. "That's why I don't like your ass."

I shook my head and rested my hand on her bare hip. "What did I do? Your crazy ass will get mad if I blink too slow."

"Shut up. I asked you a question. Like last time, you're not here with me anymore. When you do that, it makes me wonder what's got you like this. My imagination is about to have you on the other side of my door."

"I'm sorry, G. I'm listening now."

"Zakari, if we need to shut this all down, then we can. You keep zoning out on me. It's been weeks. Our arrangement is the only determining factor I see."

"No, I don't want that. I need you more now. Being around you gives me a break from the real world."

"Okay, but I'm not one of your jumpoffs. You can talk to me. It's still me."

"I hear you, G. I just don't want to taint our time together over some bullshit."

"What bullshit, Zak? You about to die or something?"

I burst out laughing. Gia didn't lie about jumping to the worst. The predicament I was in felt close to death.

"I'm not going anywhere. I'm not sick, I'm tired of…"

"What? Me?"

"Hell naw. You, for real, are the best part of my days and nights. I can't tell you enough how much this part I'd rather be my normal life. Knowing you don't want me for more than my body is my daily reminder."

"It's not even like that."

I shifted to see her face clearly. "Then what is it? We can't see each other like this outside these walls. I want more than this." I chuckled under my breath. "You got me sounding weak as fuck."

"I mean, I puts it down." She giggled. "Seriously, I understand what you mean. Nelle has been on my ass about what she suspects we're doing. I only told her you kissed me once. Now she talks about Trevor or you like she wants me to choose one."

"What?"

"Something is wrong with your sister. That ain't no secret. I will say she speaks highly of you except the part where I'm expected to break your hoe addiction. Her words. Oh, she also said you had a crush on me growing up."

I dropped my head. My sister always ran her damn mouth. "Man, whatever I had back then ain't got shit on the here and now. I am sitting in your bed with you in your birthday suit."

She blushed. "Shut up."

"Look, I want this with you like normal people, but you don't do relationships. So, where does that leave me?"

Gia fell back and stared at the ceiling. "Man, I don't know."

"How long are we supposed to sneak around? I told you what I want. The ball's in your court. I can't just have you in secret."

She closed her eyes, blowing out a long breath. "Yeah, I know that too. Zak, things between us have no doubt changed, but I'm still not sure if full-blown relationships are for me. You understand, right?"

"I really don't. You gotta do what makes you happy. If stringing me along is what does that for you then—"

"Hold up. I am not stringing you anywhere. You offered and I accepted. I told you from the start that this would make things weird and now you're only proving me right."

"Gianna, I've wanted this from day one. I don't mean having you screaming my name either." She sucked her teeth and pushed my shoulder. "For real, G. I ain't saying I'm about to ask you to marry me tomorrow, but I wanna be more than fuck potnas."

Gia slowly sat up, pulling the sheet over her breasts. The wrinkling forehead and pursed lips said she was about to reject all that I asked for. I rested my back on the headboard and stared at the wall, awaiting her next words.

"We both have a lot going on. So, maybe it's best to nip this arrangement before we complicate things further."

I wasn't about to fight her on this. She could do whatever she wanted and was too stubborn to convince otherwise.

"If that's what you want, then cool. I'ma head out."

"Okay," she said.

"A'ight." I kissed her temple and got dressed. Minutes later, I sat in my car trying to figure out what the hell just happened.

With this bullshit with Myesha, I wanted to hold on to something that made some kind of sense in my life. Gia did that for me but all that bullshit with her not wanting a relationship pissed me off.

I couldn't be mad at her while hiding the fact that the

shit I might have gotten myself into would prove her right. Having a kid with another woman while I tried to make Gia my woman was some fuckboy shit. That I was not. I had to get in front of all this before I came back to Gia.

The only thing I trusted about Myesha was science and hard facts. A DNA test would give me all the answers I needed, but we'd have to wait for the baby to be born. I prayed Gia would wait that long.

## TWENTY-THREE

# Gianna

Liv's birthday came at the perfect time. I needed the distraction from missing Zak.

Yeah. Missing. I actually missed him.

I took a page out of my mom's book and bought a cute notebook from Hobby Lobby to journal my worries away. The pen just kept going as each thought popped up in my mind. I went from being grateful to God to hating how life has been without Momma and Mimi to finally forgiving Blair and wishing I could be with Zak.

That last one made me roll my eyes as I wrote it. I wanted to spare us. The other side of me didn't mind risking it all for Zak if I could guarantee we'd be the exception. But there were no guarantees.

Everything I imagined was a guaranteed trip to the looney bin. Whenever I let my thoughts run wild, flashes of a happy life with a house and kids crashed in. Me? Married with kids and a family pet? With Zakari too?

I was slowly losing my mind. All because he'd put it on me in more ways than one. I let my guard down and allowed his lips to touch mine. I was legit crazy.

So, a day to celebrate my little sister's birthday should do the trick. It succeeded for the first hour. When there was a backyard full of kids running around, those images of someday having my own ruined shit. I shook my head almost the whole time to keep myself from being sucked into the what-if bull.

All the kids had two parents, too. It must've been nice for them. The last thing I wanted was to raise a kid on my own. I was not a superwoman like the single moms doing it. There were too many factors that kept me on track for life alone. Men did dumb shit, said dumb shit, and I wanted no parts of it on most days.

Olivia and Jonah had the dream. I prayed Blair wouldn't let them down like he did the first rounds at this thing. Plus, I liked Shana. I rooted for the two of them for all of our sakes.

What a party! Games, a magician, cake, ice cream, and expensive ass gifts from people who weren't even family. When you had a doctor dad with equally wealthy friends, it was like that. Olivia deserved it, though.

After helping them clean up, Shana and I sat by the pool and downed two bottles of wine. In all the years I'd known her, we'd never talked this much. She was the age of a cool auntie, so it felt good hanging with her. I didn't give any names of anyone I talked about. I rarely shared my personal life outside my tight circle, so Blair had better not mess this up for us.

Blair came outside with another bottle of wine. "How are my two favorite ladies doing? It must be good because I can hear y'all laughing from the kitchen."

"Really? Are we being too loud?" Shana asked.

"Not at all. The kids are asleep. I welcome the two of you bonding like this."

I rolled my eyes and turned toward them in my lounge chair. "Here he goes, making it all cheesy."

"I'm not cheesy. I appreciate good times like these."

"I know you do, baby. But we were in the middle of something."

"Oh, so now you're keeping secrets from me?" Blair gently pushed my shoulder and kissed Shana's head.

I lifted my hands. "Alright, Blair. If you must know. I've been having sex with this guy and—"

He covered his ears and made noises to drown me out. "Keep your secrets. I'm going to bed."

Shana couldn't stop laughing while refilling my glass. "That's what I thought," I told him.

"Goodnight, Gianna. You'd better not drive home tonight with all this alcohol."

"Now he wants to play daddy," I mumbled.

He rested his hands on his waist. "Must you always go there?"

"I must." I giggled at his narrowed glare. "My overnight bag is already in a guest room."

"Good. This old man is about to hit the sack so I'll see you in the morning." He kissed my forehead.

"Goodnight, Blair," I said.

His shoulder dropped as he tilted his head to the side. "Dad would suffice."

"It would if I didn't spend my first twenty years without one."

"Touché. We'll get there."

I shrugged and leaned back in my seat. Maybe, maybe not.

WHEN I GOT HOME FROM WORK, I PUT MY PLAN IN motion to watch movies and order takeout. My co-workers weren't so bad, but I was too happy to get to my weekend away from them all.

I showered, got into pajamas, hopped on the couch to find my next meal. My phone screen blocked my search with Nelle's profile picture. *What did she want?*

"I'm picking you up in an hour," Janelle said instead of the typical hello when someone answered a phone.

"For what?"

"Does it matter?"

"With you, yes! You be setting people up and shit. I'd rather be fully informed."

"You're no fun. We haven't hung out in a minute and I thought today is the perfect time."

"Only because Cameron is out of town. Don't think I can't see that you're using me since the dick jar is empty for a few days."

"Do you have to say it like that? He's more than an accessible dick. That's your thing. I love spending time with him and there's absolutely nothing wrong with that."

"Yet, you basically neglect me for him one hundred percent of the time."

"That's not true."

"I got receipts. All the texts I sent asking what you were doing and all of them ended with Cameron this and Cameron that. No, I can't today. I have plans with Cameron."

"Don't do my voice like that. I may not get to see you all the time, but we at least talk every day."

"Mmmmhmmm. That's all I get. The moment he's gone, you expect me to jump up and be ready for you. Nope. I'm busy."

"With what? Your accessible dick?"

"Fuck you."

"I'll be there at your door, so you better get ready to eat and drink and whatever we decide to do afterward. Bye."

"Who said I—" My home screen appeared. "This heffa hung up on me."

Suddenly, I wished I had a man as an excuse. The outside was the last place I wanted to be.

I hadn't seen Zak in weeks. He texted me every day to check on me, but I kept my responses short. I didn't know what to do with him. The fear of everything blowing up in my face held more weight than my desire to try with him. If shit went left, I'd have to avoid his ass. Because of Nelle, that risk became harder to accept.

Like she said, Janelle arrived on time. She'd already chosen the restaurant and planned on taking me to the movies afterward. Nelle at least said I could pick the movie.

The restaurant was nearly full. Luckily, we didn't have to wait like the bigger parties who arrived before us. We followed the hostess to our table. Before we sat down, Nelle popped a guy upside his head.

He jumped up, ready to fight. Zak's eyes grew once they met mine. "What are y'all doing here?" He sat back in his chair.

"What do people usually do when they go to restaurants, dummy? We came to eat." Nelle surveyed his table as I watched him repeatedly glance at the bar. "Who are you here with? Who's food is that?"

"Huh?" Zak's regard bounced between me and the bar. "Um...yeah. What?"

"Boy, what's wrong with you?" she asked, annoyed as we sat at our table. It was right next to his. "Zak, you okay?"

"Yeah. Um, Gia, can I talk to you?"

I shook my head and opened the menu. "We good. Nothing to talk about."

"Please. We can go outside for one minute."

"Zakari, I know you fucking lying? You said you weren't with her." Nelle brought all our attention to the bar where Zak kept watching earlier. Only he must've been checking for the bathroom entrances right next to it.

A familiar face headed straight for us. One that made my blood boil. "So this is what kept your mind so damn occupied."

"Gia, I promise you it's not what you think."

Myesha stood next to their table. "Well, well, well. If it isn't the girl who moved too slow. Guess Zaky made the right choice."

"Bitch, what?" I stood in case she jumped stupid.

"What is she talking about? You said she meant nothing." Nelle said, as if the girl wasn't standing right there.

"Yo, everybody chill." Zak raised his voice. "Gia, please let's go talk."

"Baby, you don't have to break it to her in private. We can tell them since they are family, right?" The bitch rolled her eyes at me, then smiled at Nelle. "I don't know what your brother told you, but clearly I mean more than nothing since I'm having his baby."

I tipped my head to the side, waiting for him to say something. He only shook his head before dropping it. When he looked up at me, I knew she wasn't bullshitting.

Everything suddenly made sense. The man said over and over how life hit him in ways he couldn't explain. He wouldn't tell me what it was. When I asked him to leave my place the last time, he didn't object.

Zak claimed to want more with me and now he was having a baby. All the while, I weighed my options on being with him, thinking it was a possibility. Maybe he wouldn't be the typical guy that'd break my heart. Too late for that shit now.

The most fucked up thing was that I couldn't say anything with Nelle around. While she panicked and asked them a million questions, Zak stared at me like he waited for me to say something.

Myesha ran her mouth, but I heard nothing. My labored breaths and hot skin were only the precursors. I had to get out of there to keep my cool. I excused myself and darted for the exit.

# TWENTY-FOUR

# Zakari

*FUCK!*

This shit blew up in my face with no warning. Out of all the fucking places my sister and Gia could've eaten, they'd chose this fucking restaurant. The dumbass hostess just had to seat them next to me. Why would I expect anything less with my luck with Gia?

Myesha hadn't stopped blowing me up since she told me she was pregnant. So, today I agreed to take her to eat and talk. My intentions were only to set down ground rules about communication. She needed to understand where I drew the line until I had the DNA results. As fucked up as it sounded, I wanted no parts in the pregnancy journey because I wasn't her man.

If she needed something, I'd help. None of that shit felt right. I didn't want her using me if this baby turned out not to be mine.

We'd only gotten through what I wasn't tolerating from her before ordering the food. When it arrived, she gagged and ran to the restroom. At that moment, it seemed more real. The next moment, I was face-to-face with Gia.

Myesha always got salty when it came to Gia. I tried save her from whatever Myesha might say, but in her stubborn ass fashion, she wouldn't budge. Not until those dreaded words came out of Myesha's mouth. Gia looked the same way I felt when I got the news. Nelle got sucked into a curious mode with Myesha, asking a million questions.

When she ran out, I was right behind her, ignoring Nelle and Myesha calling me. "Gia, wait up." I jogged to catch up to her power-walking ass. Even when I reached her, she kept going. "G, please let me explain."

I understood exactly how that looked from anyone's perspective. All I needed was a minute. I grabbed her wrist tight enough to stop her.

Gia spun around too fast for me to block my face. She slapped me hard. People nearby heard it and gave us their unwanted attention. The moment I willed myself to face her again, she wiped her cheeks. Fuck.

"Stay the fuck away from me. I mean it. Don't fucking talk to me again. I can't believe I almost trusted your ass."

"Hell, naw. You not about to just walk away because you don't wanna listen."

"Listen to what? The bitch is pregnant. Is that not what I heard?" she yelled.

I massaged my temples. "You need to calm the fuck down. The baby might not even be mine."

"Ohhh! Okay! That makes it okay then." She bunched her face at me. "The fuck I look like, Zakari? Go back in there with your baby mama. Ugh, all you muthafuckas are stupid as shit."

Gia took off again. I had no words. Nothing would make this any less fucked up. I followed her through the parking lot until she reached Nelle's car. She pulled the door handle to no avail.

"Fuck!" She turned around and leaned on the car. Once she lifted her head and saw me standing a couple cars away, she dropped her head back. "What are you still doing out here? Your life is in there with that woman."

"Gia, no it's not. It's with the woman I'm looking at. You're the only woman I want."

"Yet, you're about to have a baby. You can't have it both ways and there's no way in hell I'm dealing with that girl."

I moved closer to her, but not enough to get hit again. "I understand what you're feeling, Gia. Please don't let this change things between us."

"It's a child, Zakari. That's forever. I'm not doing that. Whatever we thought we had ain't worth all the drama that will come with her. She's insane or either you're lying straight to my face. The way she keeps saying you're together and now she's pregnant. How do you think that looks?"

"Gia, please don't do this."

"The only thing I'm doing is avoiding a huge mistake. You ain't no different from all the other men you claim to be nothing like." She leaned her head to the side, looking beyond me. "Good, you're here. Can we go? I wanna go home."

I turned around to find Janelle giving me that disappointed face she'd learned from our mom. When I opened my mouth to speak, she raised her hand to shut me up. Once she unlocked the car, they both got in and drove off.

I already broke my word to Gia before she gave me a chance to prove her wrong about relationships. The way this shit with Myesha came out of nowhere, that curse nonsense seemed like the only explanation for everything.

"Are you stupid or just slow?" Janelle asked the moment I opened the door. She fell onto my sofa, looking up at me to answer her.

"Nelle, you ain't gotta do all of that. I fucked up."

"That's the understatement of the century. You said this girl was crazy months ago. How the hell is she pregnant? Like for real, what's wrong with you?"

"Man, what did Gia say?"

"Nothing. She made me take her home that night and wouldn't even let me come in. It's now apparent that y'all were fucking around because she never gets like this about anyone. The fact that she's hurt means you meant something to her, and that shit is rare. Why did it have to be you, Zak? I thought you cared about her."

"I do, Janelle." I dropped into the sofa chair. "Fuck!"

"Damn, Zak. I've been on her ass for years to take someone serious. She picked your ass, then you do this?"

"Nigga, you act like I ain't livin' this shit."

"A daddy, Zak? Like really, man."

I hadn't seen Janelle in a week. You'd swear what I'd gotten myself into had something to do with her. She wouldn't talk to me because she called herself mad, too. She made me regret opening the door for her ass. I loved my sister, but damn, she got on my nerves. I could beat myself up all on my own.

"How long have you known?"

I shrugged. "A month, maybe."

"A whole month? Oh, you are officially no longer my brother. Why didn't you tell me? You keeping it a secret from everybody?"

"Dad and Byron know. They were here when she popped up and told me."

"She's been here?" She scooted to the edge of the couch. "Who are you?"

Nelle knew very well I didn't let anyone come to my place. "She's been on some stalker type shit. I never told her where I lived."

"So, you're really about to have a baby with some psycho chick?"

"Man, that shit ain't official until shorty drops the baby and a DNA test confirms it."

"Okay, so what until then?"

"I'ma wait."

"Ugh, you messed up, Zak. I don't want to be an aunt to a baby from her."

"How you made this about you? I could be the daddy. I think my dilemma trumps yours, stupid."

"You should've knocked Gia up instead."

"What?"

"I'm just saying. If you gon' be reckless, it would've been better if it was my best friend. At least we'd know what we were getting."

"Yo, something is wrong with you."

I went to the kitchen to get us both a beer. The sonogram still sat on my counter. I picked it up and brought it to her. Nelle examined the picture for a minute. Her jaw dropped before she caught the giggles.

"What's so damn funny?" I asked.

"Oh, you are dumb, dumb."

"What?"

"Did you even read the damn thing?"

"Read what? It's a picture."

Janelle tossed it to me. I noticed words and numbers that I hadn't seen before. Hell, I hadn't looked at it since the day I got it. It'd been sitting on the counter the whole time.

Myesha ran a marker over the writing, failing to hide it completely.

I read it three times. "Hold up."

"Whoever that baby is, they are like six years old right now."

"Yo, what the fuck? This ain't even real?"

"It's real. It's just not recent and definitely not yours. That bitch is not pregnant." Nelle opened her bottle and folded her legs beneath her. "The bitch is crazy, but she's not having your baby."

"Nelle, what the—"

"I'm gonna get to the bottom of this. Ain't nobody 'bout to get away with tryna pull this shit on my brother. Tell me everything about her. If she'd go this far, we need to find out what else she's capable of."

I held the cold bottle to my head. In what world could shit like this happen to me? My dad gave me the whole talk about being a responsible man and how disappointed he was with me. Thank God I still hadn't broken the news to my mom.

Janelle told me to act normal with Myesha so she wouldn't notice we knew the truth. Whatever she found out made no difference to me. I only had to clear things up with one person.

"You think Gia will talk to me?"

"Boy, that ship has sailed. She's going out with Trevor on Friday. Don't fuck this up for her. Trevor's a good man. He's exactly what Gia needs in her life."

"So, what does that make me?"

"I'm sorry. Did you not just think you got somebody pregnant minutes ago? True or not, you messed that up."

Nah. I wasn't giving Gia up that easily. She'd have to forgive me. Dude would have to fight me for her. He'd lose.

## TWENTY-FIVE

# Gianna

I HADN'T DONE THIS OFFICIALLY IN SO DAMN LONG. A man picking me up and taking me out to a classy restaurant. Just wining and dining.

After the bullshit with Zak, I welcomed the call from Trevor. Technically, I'd called him first but missed him. I'd entertain anything or anyone to keep my mind far from Zakari. Besides, it'd finally get Nelle off my back about her brother or dating.

I finished getting ready and sat at my bar with a glass of Fireball. When someone knocked, I rushed to finish my drink. He was early.

I looked out the peephole to see Trevor before he saw me. Then I hit the door. "No! Go away, Zakari."

"Gia, open the damn door."

"Hell no."

"I've been trying to reach you but yo' childish ass blocked me."

"Childish is getting random bitches pregnant. Get away from my door. I don't have time for this."

I heard another voice and looked through the peephole

again. Trevor stood next to Zakari. Oh, hell naw. I pulled the door open.

"Hey, Trevor. Let me get my shoes." I invited him in and tried to close the door, but Zak wasn't having it. I wasn't playing with him anymore.

I sat on the arm of the couch to put on my shoes. Zak stepped to me. "You lettin' niggas know where you live now?"

"Trevor is an honorable man. I'm sure I'll be safe with him."

"Safe? Is that what this is about? He makes you feel safe or is he the safe way out?"

"Zak, get out. We have plans."

"So, you really about to leave with this nigga after what we had?"

"Keyword, father-to-be. Had. As in the past, done, and over with. You should check on your baby mama, Zaky."

"Hell naw. You ain't getting off that easy. I told you what it was. You don't even have the complete story because your hardheaded ass won't listen."

"Well, I'm telling you what it is. Leave me the fuck alone. I got shit to do."

Zak's nose flared, leering at me. I kept a straight face. He finally walked out and brushed past Trevor.

"I'm so sorry about that, Trevor."

"Should I be concerned? That looked intense."

"It was nothing. I'm ready if you are."

Luckily, he shrugged it off as we walked out. Trevor asked about my day on the way to his car, like none of that even happened. I was happy he could ignore it.

He opened the passenger door for me before getting into the driver's seat. "I thought I wouldn't hear from you. What made you call?"

"Honestly, I was kind of in a situation."

"I recall asking you out and you said yes."

"You did. I did. I hadn't fully committed to the idea of entertaining the other person that night. Then things changed."

"I see."

The drive helped me relax more with him. Trevor wasn't my usual type, but I whiffed the Kool-Aid a bit with every word he spoke and subtle touches on my hand or arm.

I enjoyed Trevor's company. His kind eyes respected my body the whole time. They remained on my face or stared back at my eyes. The man had gorgeous dark moisturized skin, perfect white teeth to contrast, and a sexy goatee as the cherry on top.

The guys I involved myself with were cocky. The change was refreshing. Trevor still had the height, but his build was slimmer than my go-to type. That made no difference to me tonight because he had the brains and humor to complement his exterior.

We cruised through our entrees as he talked about his family and co-workers. He had a lot of pent-up annoyance that he hadn't released until now. I cringed at hearing the stories about people pissing him off and how he passively took it to keep the peace. I needed to practice his level of patience.

I could talk with Trevor for hours. When it was my turn to share, I gave the basics about my mom and Mimi, meeting Janelle, and work. The night couldn't have gone better. I wished they didn't set us up because with all this wine in my system, we'd be naked in another hour. Since he had ties to people close to me, that thought had to remain unrealized.

The waiter placed our desserts before us. I took one bite of my cheesecake, closing my eyes to savor its perfection.

"That good?"

"It really is. I love cheesecake."

Trevor cleared his throat and studied me for a bit. "Can I ask you something?"

"Sure."

"I like you and I'd love nothing more than to see where this could lead."

I expected that punk-ass conjunction which always came in to ruin the mood. "Okay."

"But..." And there it was. "Cameron told me you were... promiscuous. You don't seem like it, so I wanted to ask if it's true?"

Oh, this nigga couldn't be serious right now. His punk ass—because he'd officially flunked to punk ass—needed to say the exact words. In the lamest terms. "Is what true?"

He motioned his hands in a circle as if I'd say it for him. "You know. Are you a...um?"

"A virgin? I'm pushing thirty, I look like this, and I have my shit together. What do you think? I love God, but I am not Mary."

Trevor half-smiled and scratched the back of his neck. "I didn't mean a virgin. I actually meant the opposite."

"I mean that too. No, I'm not a virgin. That's what you're asking me, correct?"

I fought hard to hold back my giggles because he looked so nervous and embarrassed. Trying to ask me if I was a hoe should be more embarrassing for me.

Janelle's ass talked too damn much about everybody's business but hers. It'd be just my luck that her man did the same.

"Never mind. Sorry I asked."

"I am too. Even if you didn't exactly say the words. You're asking if I'm a hoe. On our first date that was going great until now. You chose to ask me if my body belonged to me and if I did what the fuck I wanted with it."

Trevor leaned on the backrest of his chair, holding his balled hands to his mouth. I pushed my cheesecake away and finished my wine. I kept my eyes on him to make this shit as uncomfortable as he made it. The man's eyes roved almost every visible inch of this place to avoid contact.

"Sooo, yeah. I'm gonna go."

"I picked you up." Trevor stood as I did.

I nodded. "The great thing about this day and age is that everything you need is literally at your fingertips." I waved my phone. "Except for men who respect strong women who live as freely as they do. You know the kind that aren't judgmental. Then again, you probably don't. Anyway, I hope to see very little of you in the future."

"Gianna, I'm so sorry. I promise you; I didn't mean any harm. I only—"

Raising my hand to stop him, I said, "Trevor, it doesn't matter now. I said what I had to say. Hope you find the untouched woman you want."

As I walked away, I hated how wounded I felt. My intentions weren't to fall for Trevor in one night or ever. I wanted to have a good time with a fine-ass man that wasn't Janelle's brother. It'd almost worked, but him saying dumb shit only reminded me of Zak.

That dumb motherfucker. How do you get a woman pregnant that you swore up and down you didn't mess with? How stupid could he be to do anything with her that could put him in this situation?

I wasn't saying that shit didn't happen. Why the fuck did it have to happen to Zak?

My Uber driver stared at me through her rearview mirror at almost every red light. When my phone rang, I couldn't answer it fast enough.

"Hey babe."

"Babe? Where you at?" Nelle asked.

"On my way home to you. You should know since you track my every move. The meeting went well, so the guns will be there before I am."

"Uber?"

"Yep."

"Creepy dude?"

"The other end of the spectrum but same vibes. Everybody there waiting?"

"How'd the date go? Cam is on the phone with Trevor in the other room."

"Bad enough for me to pull the trigger. The snitch's name came up. His fiancée will probably be the next target."

The driver pulled up to the leasing office. I told her ass goodbye and rushed inside the building.

"You're scared of a girl?"

"Cautious with my precious life is all. Can't be too careful. The females will do you worse than men if it meant they'd get paid. I don't trust nobody."

"True. Now what did you say about Cameron snitching? What did I do?"

I told her how the date had ended since the beginning no longer mattered. "So, the next time you run your mouth about me to your man, rethink that shit. You are *my* best friend. I don't know that fool like that. Now, I don't want to."

"Don't be like that, Gia. I'm sorry. I may have talked about your views because you frustrate the hell out of me, but I didn't call you a hoe. I'll say that to your face, not behind your back. I may have said you give yourself away though."

"Well, your man interpreted it as me being a hoe and told Trevor like he wasn't the one who set us up."

"So, that means you won't see him anymore? It's not that bad of a question. He's a good guy and I'm sure he just doesn't want to share you if it got to that point."

"Then his ass should've waited until he had a chance first."

"Sorry, girl."

"Yeah, sure."

"Sooo? Are we ever going to talk about you and my brother?"

"Nope."

"Gia?"

"Janelle. I'm not. Thank you for checking on my disaster date. Now, I need a shower and the pillow. Goodnight." I hung up before she said anything else.

I reached my hall and realized tonight would only get worse.

"Zak, why are you still here?"

My ass needed new friends.

# TWENTY-SIX

# Gianna

ZAK STOOD AFTER SITTING IN FRONT OF MY DOOR FOR who knew how long. "I need to talk to you and I'm not leaving until you listen."

"What if I didn't come home alone?"

"I still wouldn't give a fuck. That nigga ain't for you, G."

I rolled my eyes. "Who do you think you are? You're not my man. I don't care to hear anything you have to say."

"That corny nigga can get your time? Where he at, anyway? What kinda man don't walk you to your door?"

"That's none of your business. What kind of man waits for somebody after a date when they got a whole baby mama?"

I opened my door, and in Zakari's fashion, he was on my ass bum-rushing his way into my apartment. I kicked off my shoes, faced him, motioned my hand for him to get on with it. The quicker we got that done, the faster he'd get out of my space.

"How was your date?" he asked with the slightest bit of interest.

I crossed my arms over my chest, forcing all the air

through my nostrils. "Not your business. What do you want?"

"Dawg, what the hell is yo' problem? You can answer a simple question without all that damn attitude."

I said nothing. Zak got in my face, stealing my breath. I wanted to hate him; unfortunately, my body didn't get the message and reacted against my will. My nipples hardened, revealing themselves through my thin bra and top. I hadn't had this issue all night.

"Zakari, say what you gotta say so you can leave."

"Ay, your mean ass can front all you want but you can't hide everything." I slapped his hand away when he thumbed my nipple. Zak lowered his head with a chuckle. Even his damn laugh was sexy as hell. Why did the unreasonably fine ones have to be unreasonably stupid?

"I came here to tell you that Myesha lied about everything. She's not pregnant. I'm not having a baby."

"Good for you. Anything else?"

"Stop frontin'. I'm not about to lose you over shit that wasn't even real."

"You never had me to lose me, bruh."

Zak smirked and hooked my waist, pulling me into him. "Bring yo' ass. I'm not doing this shit with you, Gia. I love you."

"You what?"

He brushed his lips over mine. It pissed me off that his touch did more to me than anyone else's. After tongue fighting for a minute, I pulled away.

"You heard me, Gianna Jameson."

I stood frozen as he rested his forehead against mine. Kissing me ever so softly before lifting me to the island countertop. He bit my lip, then licked my cleavage, biting my exposed breasts. As much as I wanted to tell him to stop, I didn't.

Zak pushed me back and spread my legs as he kissed his way from my feet to my inner thigh. He bit me harder the closer he got to my middle. He kissed me through my panties, causing me to ache right where I wanted him. This shit was so unfair. I still wanted to be mad at him.

Biting my lower lips through my panties, he had me arching my back and moaning for him to have his way.

Zak yanked my panties to the side and dove tongue first into my lake. The overflow was all his doing. My body had some type of agreement with him; he'd get the most out of her.

I gripped the edge of the counter, trying my best to hold back my screams. The sound of him moaning and smacking on my love was an audible addiction.

After my second arrival, he latched onto my pussy like it was attached to his fucking mouth. When I moved, he moved.

"Ahhhh, Zaaaakkkk!" I quivered enough for him to break away. My eyes rolled back as I gained my composure.

"Come here," he whispered before scooting me to the edge and lifting me around his waist.

The heat between my legs traveled throughout my body, reminding me of how good I'd have it if I forgave him. Dammit, I wanted to.

As he walked us to the living room, I suckled his bottom lip, tasting myself. I sucked on his tongue to steal the flavor.

We stood in front of the couch until he unbuckled his belt, letting his jeans fall to his knees. The moment he sat down, we fucked up.

"Uhhh. What the..." was all I had.

"Shit, wait...fuck!"

The term "fell on his dick" was indeed possible. When he sat, my opening slid down his bare shaft. I froze for a second, then I rode him slowly. I was already in trouble because I refused to backpedal.

*Gia, what the fuck is wrong with you?*

Zak watched our connection for a few moments, then gazed at me. I stupidly nodded, giving him the okay. He gripped my neck, crashing his mouth into mine. Tongues finding their favorite dance partner, we moved in slow motion. At least that's how it felt in my mind. There was no way I was letting this nigga raw dawg me like this. I had to stop. *Gia, stop.*

"Fuck, G. What are you doing to me?" Zak's head fell back as I lifted and dropped my pussy onto his lap. I couldn't stop.

He sank his fingers into my ass cheeks, guiding my speed and pulling me onto him harder. I closed my eyes and let my head fall back. Zak wet my nipples again with his tongue and tugged on each with his teeth.

I tightened my grip on his dick, causing louder growls from his lips. The hissing of this man trying to keep his composure only made me work harder to get one more out so I could hop off. I held onto his shoulders as my body jerked. Zak let out a loud ass moan one second. The next second, the warmth of his seeds pumped into me.

I screamed and jumped off before punching his chest. "Zak, what the fuck? You just almost got somebody pregnant. No, no, no, no, no." I ran to the bathroom and tried to wash it out of me.

He knocked on the door. "Gia, let me in. I'm sorry. I wasn't tryna do that shit on purpose."

"The hell you didn't, Zakari."

"Man, I ain't ready for no baby. You ain't either. You'll be alright."

"How would you know, you dumbass? Is that what you been doing? Fucking girls raw and thinking nothing will happen 'cause you don't want it to?"

"Gia, I never did that shit before. I just got lost in it."

"Get out!"

"G, come on, man."

"Get the fuck out!"

I remembered I had a Plan B pill somewhere in this bathroom. Birth control was in effect, but this could still go south fast. Although I did nothing without protection, I bought Plan B in case of an emergency. I found it under the cabinet and checked the expiration date. It still had one more year left.

I rushed to the kitchen, wrapped in my robe. When I passed my living room, I jumped and dropped the damn box. "Zak, I told you to leave."

"Not until I know you're okay. You gotta lock the door behind me, anyway."

"Ugh, now you wanna be cautious."

"I'd take a baby over some psycho motherfucker hurting you."

"Whatever." I got a glass of water and opened the box. After briefly reading the instructions, I took the pill.

Zak watched the whole time with no words. He looked sorry, but it was both of our faults. He made me do stupid shit. The more reason to nip this completely.

"I'm out now. I'll lock it. You need to leave."

"Gia, stop tryna push me away. I wanna be here with you. I wanna be with you, period."

I shook my head. "We can't. I'm not myself when I'm

around you and I can't have that. You make everything so confusing, Zak. I need something different."

"Something or someone?"

"Just...not...you."

His bottom lip disappeared into his mouth as he nodded repeatedly. "So, you're for real. After everything we just did, after what I said, you still won't even try."

"Zak, I have tried. You make me crazy and I don't want to be that way."

"Is it ol' dude?"

Zak would soon find out from Janelle's news reporting ass. I still took it as a way out, at least for tonight.

"Yes. I'm gonna see him again and maybe even date him for real."

"In a relationship?"

The way he asked me that question made my eyes more sensitive to the air. I didn't want to hurt him any more than I didn't want to get hurt.

"Yes," I barely got out.

Zak pressed his lips together, scratching his brow. "A'ight, Gianna. I hope you find what you've been looking for. I can't lie and say this ain't some bullshit, but I'm not about to force yo' ass either."

"Good."

Zak exhaled heavily. I wanted to run to him, jump in his arms, and take back everything I said. I wanted to let go of every single reservation. He'd be everything I needed because he knew how to handle me. Zak could also royally fuck me over with shit like this Myesha situation. It was already too much.

He walked over to me and lifted my chin, forcing me to look into his eyes. "I still love you." He kissed me and finally exited.

The second the door closed, I let out the breath I held. My vision blurred and my cheeks were soaked. I broke my number one rule: never fall for any man.

Being with Zak was too dangerous. I had risked my heart and my freedom after allowing him in.

# Zakari

Bᴀᴍ. Bᴀᴍ. Bᴀᴍ.

Either the police were at my door or Janelle's heavy-handed ass was. I jerked it open and found the latter.

"You really need to stop knocking on my door like that. I got neighbors."

Nelle sucked her teeth. "And? You got something to drink?" She asked on her way to the fridge.

"Yeah. What's up witchu? Cameron needs to catch these hands or something? I been wanting to knock his ass around for a minute."

"You cannot still trippin' about him hooking Gia up with Trevor."

"The reason don't matter."

"Whatever. I just left Myesha's baby daddy." Janelle air quoted baby daddy.

I took the beer she handed me after she sat beside me. "Why the hell you meeting with people by yourself?"

"Boy, I'm grown."

"You had your gun, didn't you?"

"Hell, yeah. I ain't crazy. We were outside the gym so there were plenty of people around."

"Good girl. How did you find him?"

"People put all their business on social media. It took only a few clicks to find out where he'd be. After you pointed him out on her Facebook page, everything else came easy. The dude she said was her baby daddy is actually her brother."

"What?"

"Yup. She ain't got no kids. She has a niece, though. Her brother was pissed when I told him what she did. He gave me the whole rundown of her wanting to have a family. Every guy she messes with, she becomes obsessed. You were simply her current target. The way her brother told it, she might have some mental issues because she will imagine entire relationships with guys, then go to them as if they were aware. The girl done had multiple restraining orders against her." Janelle patted me on the back. "What a way to pick 'em. This one takes the cake, Zak."

"I guess so. I might have to file papers on her ass too."

"I hope this shuts it down."

"Me too."

Nelle and I came up with a plan to put this to rest. I texted Myesha to meet up.

"Oooh, I can't wait to see her lying ass face when it's done," my sister said with her own sinister smile. "We need to tell Gia about this. The whole thing is insane." She picked up her phone.

I slapped it out of her hand. She slapped me upside my head in return. "What the hell, stupid?"

"Yo' ass messy."

"Nigga, please. Stop acting like you don't wanna tell

her." She mushed the side of my head. "That's what you get for always screwing any woman who'd let you."

"Now, the only one I wanted is with another nigga. Ain't no point no more."

"Aww, you sound so wounded." She tried to mush me again, but I dodged it and pushed her over. "Stupid. They went on one date. You act like they're in a full-blown relationship."

"Whatchu mean one date? Gia said she was with ol' dude now."

"On their first date, she got mad at him for asking if she was a hoe. From what I understand, Gia hasn't seen him since."

"He asked her that?" I chuckled.

"Yeah. She blamed me for talking to Cameron about her. I wasn't trying to bash her or anything but when Gia believes something, it'd take a miracle to convince her otherwise."

"You ain't never lied."

Janelle's phone chirped. "That's her now."

"What does she want?"

"Uh, nothing to do with you."

I smacked my lips and let it go until she put her phone down. I grabbed it and read the text.

**Gia: He's here. I'll text when he's gone. If I don't call you tonight, you got the address.**

I scrolled up, finding a link to a hotel's address. My sister's short arms reached around me but didn't get anywhere close to her phone. I recognized a name and immediately gave the phone back.

"You play too much. I told you it wasn't your business."

My head throbbed as my palms moistened. Gia went back to her old ways. I remembered the guy's name from the bar. That disrespectful ass nigga was about to have his hands all over her. It irked me more than the Trevor dude.

For the life of me, I couldn't understand how the shit she did was anywhere near better than being with me. Things almost got fucked up with Myesha, but that was dead. Gia had no excuse besides being hardheaded. I was tired of trying to make her see what we could have. Having me sounding soft for her ass also grew old when she showed nothing in return.

"You read all of that? You okay?"

"Man, I'm chillin'. You staying to eat or what? I'm about to order some food."

"Yeah, I can stay."

My sister's voice was laced with pity. I didn't need it. I knew what I had to offer when the time came for me to be with one woman. Until then, back to the regularly scheduled program.

Nelle kept her eyes on me. "You seem mad."

"I'm good."

"Zak, you ain't gotta front with me."

"Janelle, you're annoying as fuck. I told you I'm good."

"Okay with yo' big head ass."

"That's why these females stay on it."

She scrunched her face. "What?" I assumed she caught on when she gasped. "Eww! You nasty."

"They like that about me too."

Janelle dramatically gagged. "I cannot with you. Please, stop talking."

"You be in my business, anyway. You might as well hear why your brother gets so much pus—"

Nelle screamed and threw a pillow in my face. I laughed so hard my side hurt. She hated when I said it.

"I really hate you."

"Yeah, whatever. You can go home, you mud duck."

She cracked up. "Fuck you."

We chilled for two hours. Janelle's phone interrupted the movie. The conversation she failed to have in private ruined my mood for the night. I told her I had a headache and wanted to shower and go to sleep. I was sure she read right through it, but obliged and left me alone.

I had to cleanse myself of Gia.

---

LAST NIGHT, I HIT UP TYRA. SHE MADE ALL MY DUMB ass feelings go away. Temporarily. Girlie gave me head for the imaginary trophy. For a second, I internally laughed at when Gia had tried to do it one night.

Gia complained about not getting her mouth around me good. The fact I came quicker than I did last night said otherwise. That was when I realized the person mattered more than the act. Plus, Gia was better at everything else.

After Tyra gave me what I needed, I took my ass home. The drive did more harm than good. My mind would not get off the one woman who didn't want me the same. She should've kept her ass in Florida.

Today, I'd close the door on my latest issue. I pulled up to the restaurant and found the table where Myesha waited for me. She stood when I approached her with the broadest smile I'd ever seen on her face. For a split second, I felt terrible about what I had planned.

"Hey, Zaky!" She opened her arms to receive me.

"I told you to stop calling me that shit." I hugged her so she wouldn't suspect anything. I texted her earlier that I wanted to make sure she was doing okay with the pregnancy.

"I'm sorry, Zakari. I usually have a nickname for people. We'll find something else that you will like."

It took everything in me not to crack up at her, poking her stomach out. She rubbed it a few times and played as if she was tired. She ordered water and told the waitress we were expecting. The woman congratulated us before leaving the table.

My sister messaged me she was only five minutes away. Myesha talked about morning sickness and how everything smelled so strong to her.

"I heard so much about these symptoms, but I hoped it wouldn't be as bad for me. I might not eat since I can barely keep anything down."

"Oh, yeah?"

"Yes. This is way worse than I imagined."

"I can agree with you there."

Her brows furrowed. "What do you mean?"

I pulled my wallet from my pocket and took out the ultrasound photo. I watched Myesha swallow hard as if she already understood where this was going.

"You still have that?"

"Why wouldn't I? It's my first child."

"Yeah, that makes sense. Well, I can take it and have it framed or something. It's my only copy. I didn't mean to leave it with you. I need it back to make a copy for myself."

I shook my head. "Nah, I wouldn't want the details to get any more distorted."

"Oh?"

"Yeah." I faced the picture her way and pointed at the permanent marker covering the patient's name and date. "You see? These details may get messed up even more if I give it back." Her eyes lowered to the table. "Can you see it? Because I almost missed it."

"Zakari."

"Look at me, Myesha." She did. "If you look closely, you'd notice this picture is years old and doesn't even have your name on it."

"Zakari, it's not what you think."

"Cut the shit, Myesha. You tried to play me."

"No, I didn't. I am pregnant with your baby. You have to believe me." She reached across the table for my hand. I pulled it away.

I scoffed and shook my head. "I almost did. I lost someone who really mattered to me because of it too."

She rolled her eyes and chuckled. "Is that why you are calling me a liar? Because of that Gia bitch?"

"Watch yo' fuckin' mouth, Myesha."

"For what? You're the one who said she was your family. Now you're accusing me of lying so you can be with her. What about the mother of your child?"

"You are a piece of work." I laid eyes on the very people I endured this bullshit for. I waved for them to meet us at the table.

Myesha turned toward the entrance and froze for a second. She looked back at me; lips tight like she'd hurt me if she wanted to.

"Wuzzup, Nelle. Who do you have with you?" I asked with all the bad acting to rub it in.

Janelle smiled, playing along. "Hello there, my dear brother. Guess who I ran into on the way in. He kinda resembles a baby daddy, doesn't he? Then again, he looks more like someone's brother. Hmm, I wonder how those titles can get confused?"

"Okay, we all get it. Y'all can stop," Myesha said.

"Whatever do you mean?" Nelle clutched her imaginary pearls. She looked at me. "What? Was that too much?" She snickered. "My bad."

"Marlon, what are you doing here?" Myesha asked her brother.

"He probably wants to talk about the daughter you two share. You said he was your baby's daddy. You remember, right? The one who treated you so bad that you ended up in my..." I stopped and put myself in Marlon's shoes. I wouldn't want to hear this about my sister. "You lied about all of it and the pregnancy."

"I can't believe you pulled this bullshit again, Myesha. We talked about this." Marlon crossed his arms over his chest. "I'm telling Mom this time. This has to stop."

"No! Please don't." Myesha stood with her original flat abdomen. "Marlon, this was different. He said he loved me."

"No, the hell I didn't," I defended.

"Well, you made me feel loved every time we made—"

Marlon raised his hands to stop her. "Ay, ay. Spare me the details. You were wrong to try this again. Didn't your divorce teach you anything?"

"Divorce?!" Nelle and I damn near yelled.

"I didn't tell you she succeeded with one guy, but he found out the pregnancy was a scheme," Marlon willingly told us.

"It wasn't a scheme. Stop telling all my business." Myesha hit her brother on his shoulder.

"Wow, Myesha. That's low. You were gonna try to trick me into marrying you over a fake pregnancy. Eventually, I would've noticed there was no baby."

She sucked her teeth. "That can be dismissed with a miscarriage." She covered her mouth.

"You are sick. Women really suffer from losing babies.

Why would you even play like that?" Janelle asked. "You shouldn't do this to people."

"I'm thirty-four. I'm running out of time. So, it's not a game for me."

"You said you were twenty-seven. Damn, is your name really Myesha?" I asked, expecting nothing. Her brother repeatedly shook his head like she embarrassed him. I would've been if Nelle pulled this.

Janelle's demeanor softened. "Myesha, you still have time. But God ain't gon' reward you for scamming men."

"What the hell would you know? You got a ring on your finger?"

"Look bitch, I was tryna be nice but keep playing with people and next time they won't be as understanding or forgiving. I hope you get everything you deserve." Nelle took my hand and pulled me away from the table.

On the way out, Marlon said something to Myesha that had her cussing him out. I walked out without another word.

Janelle gave me the big sister talk like we weren't only a year apart. I was careful with every woman I dealt with. Stupidity occurred only once with Gia. It wouldn't happen again.

# TWENTY-EIGHT

## Gianna

Nothing I tried worked. Not a damn thing.

I'd tried meditation, masturbation, and nightly libations. Every waking moment, Zak occupied my thoughts.

Every moment I wondered if I'd done the right thing, breaking things off with him. I wrestled with the fact that those three words he said to me were reciprocated.

I even tried the typical get under a new man to get over the old one. Technically, Troy had a go-around with me a couple times, yet he still qualified as a stranger.

That. Shit. Didn't. Work.

All I saw was Zak. I compared every stroke, the depth, the stretching of my walls, filling them beyond capacity. Nothing compared to that man. Troy was good at what he did, but Zak was better. Zak was Zak.

I was wrong about lying to him about Trevor. It didn't last long since he texted me he knew. Janelle was about to lose her spot in my go-to pocket. Things I told her never stayed between us. Another check on the con list. If I was with Zak, I couldn't tell her anything about it. He'd learn everything before I even finished a damn sentence.

The last time with Troy, I played music because I didn't want to hear his voice. I kept my eyes closed and imagined he was Zak. By the time we finished, I had given up. I told Troy we wouldn't see each other again; he shrugged and said okay. There had to be another way to flush the man out of my system.

Luckily, two of my Miami girls were coming for a visit. I talked to them on a regular but hanging with them was a whole other vibe. I'd missed them so much and welcomed the distraction.

***

"I SEE YOU BALLIN'!" TRISH SAID FOR THE THIRTY millionth time. My wardrobe had changed little since they'd last seen me. She overexaggerated as usual. My closet was a beauty, but she'd seen it all before.

"Shut up. Y'all ready to go?"

"Girl, I don't know what Lonnie's ass is doing. She's been in that bathroom for almost an hour."

"Must've been Gringo's. She knows she can't eat all that cheese with her lactose intolerant ass."

"Her knowing it won't make her stop. The girl loves dairy and creamy foods. We will never get her to understand that her body doesn't."

We laughed. "Crazy." I chose a pair of shoes and sat on my bed to put them on.

"Sooo, you ever gonna tell us anything about this new guy. Are we gonna meet him?"

"Trish, there's nothing to tell."

"If I recall, which I do very well, you said specifically that you might have to turn in your playa card. Those were your exact words. If things changed, what happened?"

Okay, I may have mentioned Zakari to the girls in our group texts. His name never came up; however, the situation was too good not to share. Janelle's ass wouldn't get the pleasure of hearing me gush about her brother.

"Like you said, things changed. On to the next. Rather, back to the old. I almost saw the light."

Trish laughed. "Something is really wrong with you. Your family is not cursed and I know you'll use this failed attempt as another check on your list."

"Don't start with me, Trish."

"Ugh, we were rooting for you and this mystery man."

"Well, root for me to find a new nighttime boo tonight."

"Oh, so you're looking for a new trainer."

I smirked at her attempt to be a smart ass. "Yep, and he can train this pu—"

"Aht! Don't even." Trish covered her ears. "Do better. Don't go back. Let our hoe days be in the past."

"Hoe?" That word had never bothered me before. If that's what people saw from my grown-ass living my grown-ass life, that was on them. Ever since Trevor had assumed, it made my body heat to the point of defense or retaliation. "Fuck you, I ain't no hoe. I'm grown and don't want one man to hold on to until he gets tired and does what the fuck he wants."

"Whoa! Why are you doing all that? When the hell did you get all sensitive?"

I raised my hand. "My bad. Shit's just been insane. My mind is all over the place."

"Apparently. And fuck you too."

"Why y'all fucking each other? What happened?" Lonnie finally appeared.

I lifted my palm to her. "First, I hope you had the fan on in there. You gon' have the whole place funky."

Lonnie chuckled. "If only it smelled the same way it went in."

"She so damn nasty. I've been stuck with her for almost a month now," Trish reminded me.

"My credit got me fucked up. Them deposits got me fucked up too."

"Lonnie, it ain't like you broke. Just pay for it. You'll most likely get it back."

This girl shrugged. "No. I'm waiting for my aunt to move into her new house. She's gonna rent her old one out to me."

"That shit will take another two months. Gia, I can't take it. She has to go."

"All the free food you eat. I cook for you and buy all the groceries."

"True dat. They ain't building that house fast enough. You gotsta go."

I cracked up at the back and forth. The living arrangement was a major topic of Trish's private texts to me. Lonnie wasn't the best roommate. On the flip side, the chick could throw down in the kitchen. That was the only trade-off.

"Y'all will survive. Now let's go so we can get in free."

I needed this night with my girls. No Janelle, no Zak.

---

"THAT MOTHERFUCKER KEEP ACCIDENTALLY BUMPING into me with this dick. If he does it again, I'ma take him to the restroom and show him something," Trish said after pointing out this fine ass dude chilling in a private section.

"You are such a hoe," Lonnie yelled over the music as it transitioned to a banger.

Trish swagged her neck left and right before lifting her hand to her hip. "Yep. Horniness Over Everything. At least until something better comes around. He better stop igniting my flame before his ass gets burned."

"Messing with him will get your ass burned and a ticket to the clinic. Watch out for that type," I warned, sipping away at my drink.

We'd been at this club for over an hour. My feet had sent me the message that we had less than an hour left. That was my fault for listening to Trish. She was on the low end of the ruler and wore heels made for one profession.

I let her talk me into wearing a pair of her more modest shoes, even at five extra inches added to my height. Although the air was fresher up here, I was a few drinks away from holding them in my hand for the rest of the night.

Trish and Lonnie leave tomorrow, so this was going to be a long but fun night. Last night, we hit up a strip club. My first time going to one at home. I'd become a regular at a few clubs with these girls, but Janelle didn't party like my Miami peeps. I thought for sure they'd be worn the hell out like I was.

In the four days they'd been here, we went everywhere they wanted. Long ass, ridiculous lines at the Turkey Leg Hut, hours at the Galleria. Whatever was on their vacation bucket list got checked off. I was so ready to drop their asses off at Bush Intercontinental.

Back on the dance floor, all eyes were on us. Rightfully so. Lonnie and Trish were stacked and racked right. We'd made it a point to make our presence known, but not be too approachable. Only the bold came to any of us. I turned a few down, especially the ones who'd offered to buy my drinks. I could do that myself and for damn sure didn't want a puppy following me around thinking that one drink was their invisible leash.

I wanted freedom tonight. Unless someone worth my time later came along, he might get my alternative number. Google gave out free numbers. Why not put them to use?

Eyes were on us, but I felt stalked. That feeling you got when someone watched you too damn hard. If I had food, it'd be on the floor right now because of whoever it was. The dimmed lights helped little when I scanned the room. With my luck, Zak's faux baby mama might pop out of a corner. Whoever it was, they needed to stay in the shadows.

After five songs into this bout sweating it out on the dance floor, someone grabbed me from behind and kissed my neck. I tried to bump him back, so I'd have room to face him. He had some damn nerve rolling up on a stranger like that. My reaction also depended on how he looked. Don't judge me.

The guy held on tight, pulling me away from my girls. Their backs were to me.

I struggled enough to elbow his side. "Ouch. Damn, Eve! I just want to dance."

Fucking D'Mario. This was worse than seeing Myesha's ass. "Well, I don't. Keep your fucking hands off me, dumbass."

"You okay?" Lonnie stepped up to us with Trish behind her. "Do we need to rearrange a nigga's face in this bitch?"

I waited to let him answer her because I was still on the fence. D'Mario scowled. "Yo' ass is crazy. I was tryna see what's up."

"Nothing is. Our last encounter should've told you that." I rolled my eyes, walking away. He caught my arm with a grip that got him popped in the face. I knew how to break a nose in one move. Thanks to my Miami trainer boo. However, D'Mario might have only suffered a swollen eye.

"Bitch, what the fuck?!" he yelled.

Trish and Lonnie squared up in case it went that far. I was ready to fight for all the shit I'd held in. I had time today.

From the corner, someone pushed their way through the crowd. I figured it was security coming to throw our asses out.

D'Mario looked at the big ass dude that showed up and chuckled. "Captain Save-a-Hoe back at it. What you wanna do? I won't hit a bitch but we can go, nigga."

I turned to see the security guy and immediately wanted to disappear. The anger in his eyes damn near scared me. I grabbed Trish and Lonnie's hands and led the way to the damn door.

"Wait, wait! I gotta close my tab," Trish said.

"Ugh. Hurry up. I need to get the fuck outta here."

"We'll wait here." Lonnie leaned against the wall near the bar. "Get some water too."

Trish nodded and left. Lonnie pushed off the wall. "I think we 'bout to get tossed on our ass. The security is heading for us. That nigga fine though. I can probably make some type of arrangement."

"We're leaving, anyway." I turned away, ready to let whoever approached us know we wouldn't be a problem. The moment I laid eyes on him, my heart and brain clashed. "Zakari."

"Gianna." The man's eyes embraced and undressed me at the same time. I wanted to run to him and let his arms do the same, but fairy tales didn't exist in my life.

"Gianna?" Lonnie repeated. "Oh, he know you, know you. Who the hell is this?"

"Nobody," I answered, still unable to break from his gaze.

"So, I'm nobody now?"

I shrugged. Zak snorted and nodded. "Lemme talk to you for a minute."

"No! I'm here with my girls and I'm not leaving them."

Trish joined Lonnie beside me. "Um, what's going on? We getting kicked out for real?"

"Shh. He's not security. I think this is the guy," Lonnie thought she whispered.

"Ohhhh, shit. *The* guy. Damn, he fine."

"Ain't he though."

"Damn, y'all. We can hear you," I told them before they giggled and Zak smirked.

Lonnie smacked her lips. "Well, hell, we can wait in the car."

"We need to talk about your butt behind your back, anyway. Up here talking about it's over. We see y'all. Whatever it is, it sure as hell ain't over," Trish claimed. "If you leave with him, let us know so we can take your car to your place."

"Oh, and don't worry about taking us to the airport if you sleep over. We can get a ride," Lonnie added.

"First, your flight is in the afternoon. Second, I'm not leaving with him. We can go right now. I have nothing to say to him."

They looked at each other, then back at me. "Stop being stupid. We'll be in the car," Lonnie said.

Trish waved at Zak. "Nice to kind of meet you. I'm sure we will get a formal introduction some other time."

"Right. Like at the wedding." Lonnie winked like any of what they said meant anything.

"Or the baby shower. Look how he looking at her. She

getting pregnant tonight." Trish didn't help either. Both of them were on the same dumb shit tonight.

"I swear on everything I hate y'all."

"We love you too. Bye." Just like that, they left the building. The only thing keeping me behind was Zak's arm draped across my waist. He caught me when I attempted to walk out after them. I didn't fight him. My brain lost that one.

# TWENTY-NINE

# Zakari

To think I'd sulked all day and tried to pass on coming here. Byron wanted to celebrate his promotion. I'd declined twice until he showed up at my apartment. It took him a half-hour to motivate me to get off the couch.

The moment Gia strolled in with those two women, I sensed her. My regard traveled straight to her and hadn't left her the whole night. I didn't want to be there, so I had the excuse of just chilling in our section and watching from a distance. Byron had Trina; the other guys latched on to women on the dance floor, leaving me alone like I preferred.

Gia wore skin-hugging black jeans, a dark top with long necklaces hanging past her breasts, and heels that gave her false average height. Her short ass looked good as hell. Everything that pissed me off about her disappeared. That woman was mine.

A few dudes tried to buy her drinks, but each one got the head shake. She was on her independent shit tonight. I remember her telling me how much she hated when men bought drinks and thought it meant they had bought her for the night. We used to joke about that. Witnessing it play out only made me want to leave my spot to get her. Gia played hard better than anyone.

The women with her were just as fine and turned down just as many guys. When they danced, all eyes were on them. Sometimes they'd let niggas catch a feel when the right song came on. That shit had my blood boiling. Gia only danced with two dudes and not for long. It was long enough for me to keep my eyes on them afterward. They might try to get at her after one minute of dancing. Gia had that type of pull.

My friends returned to the section, each coupled up. They pushed for me to do more than sit. Byron and Trina double-teamed me with the whole genuine relationship bullshit when I glimpsed a familiar face in the crowd. He reached Gia and held onto her like I would. For a second, I thought she'd gone back to messing with that trash nigga. The moment she saw him, that notion was proved wrong.

When he grabbed her, I made my way to the dance floor with quickness. That motherfucker had laid his hands on her for the last time. By the time I reached them, she had handled him. Gia laid eyes on me and took off. Her little nigga fronted like he'd do something, but backed down when I stepped to him. A bouncer stood next to me, making sure there wasn't a problem. I reassured him and followed where I thought Gia had run off to.

Once her friends left us alone after giving me insight into their conversations about me, I knew this was a done deal. Gia's hardheaded ass felt the same thing I did. Her mouth tried to say otherwise, but her body always gave her away. I noticed the uptick in her breathing, the gloss over her eyes when she looked at me, and her nipples tryna tell me to taste them.

"Stalking me now?"

I scoffed. This woman couldn't help herself. She always had a smart-ass comment. "Never. I don't have to. You'll always come to me."

"Boy, please. Ain't nobody come for you."

"Yet, here you are."

"Pure coincidence."

Some people passed by to leave. We moved over to get out of the way.

"Yo' boy? Was that a coincidence or are you fuckin' him again?"

"No, I'm not!" she said with disgust. "Not that it's any of your damn business. You still back to your rotation."

"Not the full schedule, but yeah." Gia's eyes pierced me like that was the wrong answer. "What? You thought I'd wait on your stubborn ass. You don't want me, remember?"

"I don't."

"Then why you bothered?"

"I'm not."

"Right. You meeting niggas in hotels again."

"I've been minding my grown ass—"

My mouth covered hers. I didn't feel like going back and forth with her ass when we both knew how this would end. She'd talk shit, I'd reciprocate, and so on.

The rest of the building vanished for the moments we connected. All the shit we said to each other that contradicted this right here didn't matter at all. Gia needed to get her ass in line with what I already knew. My life was with her. I wasn't a nigga that dreamed of having a white picket fence, three kids, and a dog. Gia made me envision all those corny images with her.

I promised that if I got her, that'd be it. Everything my family wanted for me was in Gia's hands. None of the women I messed with gave me visions of anything further than the night with them. This woman had me seeing a whole damn future I claimed I didn't want.

I released her after almost a minute of getting reacquainted with her tongue. Searching her eyes, I knew this was the last time we'd have this damn conversation. "I love you."

Gia groaned as she searched my eyes. Then she rolled hers and said, "I love you too." She appeared defeated. Luckily for me, she'd stopped fighting the truth.

"'Bout damn time."

Gia laughed. "I still don't like you."

"That's only 'cause I don't take your shit."

"Whatever."

I pulled her into me and kissed her ear before asking, "Sooo, you talk about me to your friends?"

Gia hit me. "Shut up. I may have mentioned this asshole who wouldn't leave me alone."

"The same motherfucker is over there somewhere waiting for you to be alone so he can strike again. That's your real stalker. If I see him again, I'm beating his ass. He talks too much shit."

"He really does. Even while he's—"

"You better not finish that fucking sentence."

She burst out laughing. "Aww, is Zaky jealous? You're the one with baby mamas."

I sucked my teeth. "I don't have no damn baby mama. At least not yet. Depending if that Plan B worked."

Her eyes ballooned. "That shit ain't funny, Zakari."

I laughed at her pouting face. "Stop being a baby. You will have my baby, eventually."

"You wish."

"I do."

"Then you better not do anything stupid. If I do this all the way with you, I will fuck you up if you fuck me over."

"I'm definitely gonna fuck you over. Over the counter, the couch, the balcony too. But I will never hurt you. You can officially call that damn curse of yours broken because you got me. It's a done deal."

"Yeah, we'll see about that."

WHEN I PULLED UP TO OUR BUILDING, GIA'S FACE twisted up. "I thought we were going to your place."

"We are."

"Then why arc we here?"

I grabbed my rcmote and opened the garage door. Gia still tried to make sense of it.

"What's on your mind?" I asked.

"Did you steal my fob again?"

"What?"

"Janelle told me she caught you with my key and took it back. I wondered how you always ended up at my door without access to the building."

I shook my head and laughed. "Yo, my sister is a damn blabbcrmouth for real. Damn. I can't trust her for shit."

"Nah, you can trust that she will run her damn mouth. I mean, it is what it is."

"True."

"So, again, sir. Did you take it back?" Gia tried to take the remote from me.

I smacked my lips. "This right here is mine." I parked as she turned her head in every way possible.

"Zak, this is the wrong floor."

"Just get yo' fine ass out of the car."

Surprisingly, Gia obliged. A rarity for her always-fighting-me ass. I took her hand and walked to the entrance of my hall. One floor beneath hers.

I walked behind her, pulling her into me to slow our pace. Gia leaned her back onto my chest, looking up at me. I kissed her intensely. Inhaling her, savoring her, preparing her.

Gia moaned, slowing her steps almost to a halt. I bumped her ass with my middle so we'd continue down the empty hall. Peeking ahead to make sure no one turned a corner; I slid my hand down her belly and stopped at the entrance of her jeans.

"Boy, you better stop," Gia whined.

She faced forward, guiding my hand. I knew she was fronting. My baby widened her legs as we continued to walk a few more feet. I dug deep enough to find her wet heat. Gia gasped and froze. "Wait, don't they have cameras in the halls?"

"I don't give a fuck."

"Where are we going? I live upstairs."

I kept my hand on her love and used the other to unlock the door we'd stopped in front of.

"Zak, what are you doing?"

"Taking you home like I said."

Gia acted like she didn't believe me until the door opened. Her ass just stood in the doorway, peeking inside. I didn't want to answer any more questions tonight. I pushed my fingers inside of her to distract her and guide her steps.

The moment the door shut behind us, I yanked her pants down before lowering mine. After covering myself, I replaced my fingers with something more filling. Gia's sounds filled my half-unpacked apartment.

"Shit!" she screamed as I gripped her shoulder and her waist, pulling her pussy onto me hard.

"I told you I would fuck you over the counter, the couch, and the balcony. That's what the fuck we 'bout to do."

# THIRTY

## Zakari

"Awww, look at the happy couple!" Janelle met us on our way to everyone gathered under the gazebo. "Ooooh, we should have a double wedding!"

Gia cut her eyes at my sister. "Girl, if you don't get yo' over-eager, messy ass out of my face. You are the only one walking down the aisle."

"I'm saying. Let us live, man. You always doing too damn much." I shoved Janelle over a bit.

My sister scrunched her face like something confused her. "At the brunch with Shana, Gia said she could see herself marrying you, little brother. You better take me to pick out the ring."

"Nelle!" Gia and I said. We'd grown tired of her ass already and we'd just gotten here.

"To think I stole your key back for you," Gia told Janelle.

Janelle nodded slowly. "You right, you right. My bad, girl. I'm just too happy that you both got yourselves together."

I glanced down at my baby. "What key?"

"The one you use for everything but emergencies." Nelle shoved my arm.

I pulled my keys from my pocket and the key to my sister's apartment was indeed missing. "When did you do that? We're sneaking and taking stuff now?"

Gia's looked at me like I was crazy. "I'm sorry, this coming from the guy who stole my extra key fob from his sister's car."

"Touché. In my defense, I confessed."

"Was that before or after you got caught?" Janelle jumped in. "You didn't think I'd tell her?"

"Of course, I did, Babbling Belinda." I flicked her forehead.

Janelle swung at my head and missed. We took a stance for our slap fighting routine. Before we could go at it, Mom called me to come over.

"Saved by yo' momma," she said. Janelle walked to the kids playing dodgeball.

We had a ton of cousins, which was why we had our family cookouts at parks. It was too many of us to cram into somebody's house.

These gatherings happened maybe twice a year outside of family-oriented holidays. All we needed was a banner for this to be a full-out family reunion.

My dad and his siblings went at it with my mom's brothers in the Battle of the Ribs contest. My aunts competed with the desserts and sides. We had cards to fill out for the best-tasting competitor and dropped them in the bowls next to the dish. The winners got a gift card with a healthy amount of hundreds on it. They didn't play about it either.

The entire day was comprised of good food, games for adults and children, and a few sports competitions between the young and old. The old men in the family wouldn't back down because they beat us one year at basketball. Either way, it was the best time every time.

Byron and Trina beat us here. He always got an invitation so my dad could claim two sons when we battled my cousins on whatever was on the itinerary. The two of them met us on the way to my mom and aunts. I welcomed another distraction before we faced the women of my family.

"I won't say much more than the truth. Y'all look good together," Byron gushed. He got on my damn nerves with his cheesing ass.

"Y'all really do," Trina seconded.

Gia looked up at me. I kissed her. "Thank you," I said.

She narrowed her eyes. "Who? Me or them?"

"Both." I couldn't do anything but smile with this woman on my arm. "You especially. I'll personally thank you later."

"Damn, Gia." Byron sounded like Martin's famous line. "You got him all affectionate and shit. Y'all gon' be like us soon."

Byron nodded at Trina. She raised her left hand near her face to show off the diamond on that ring finger. "Ohhh, shit. You did it already?" I asked B. He told me he'd gotten the ring; he didn't say when he'd propose.

He shrugged before pulling his lady closer. "I couldn't wait. When you're sure, you gotta set it in stone."

"Congratulations! Your ring is beautiful," Gia told Trina, who smiled nonstop.

"Thank you."

"Like I said..." Byron cleared his throat. "Y'all next."

"Bruh, you two been together for a couple of years. We only got a couple months in. Chill with all of that."

"Not if you count all the years you crushed on her. Y'all damn near on y'all fifteenth anniversary in your mind," Byron threw out there to clown me.

I couldn't help but laugh. It used to be embarrassing for Gia to hear about my childhood crush. I had her now. "You a fool. We good. Lemme go see my mom. She looks like she's talking about us."

"Everybody's on it today, huh?" Gia laughed and rolled her eyes.

"I'm saying." We continued our stroll to the women's table. I squeezed Gia's hand. "You nervous, baby?"

"Kind of. It's not like I don't know your family. It is a little weird though. All this time we spent around each other, who knew it'd continue with me as your woman."

"Shit, I did." She nudged me. "Not until you came back, at least. Before, it was still a bit of a fantasy. I figured I'd have to break your hard ass down. Didn't think it'd be this damn hard, but I ain't no quitter."

"Mmhmm. I guess we are really doing this. Damn, why are they staring at us like that? Your momma is smiling at us too damn hard."

"Yeah, she 'bout to clown. I can feel it. We can make a run for it."

"Boy, I ain't scurred."

"Yeah, I forget you a thug."

"Shut up."

The table fell quiet when we reached it. "Hey, Ma!" I hugged her. "What's up, Grandma? Whuddup, aunties!" I went down the row on both sides, giving each woman a hug. Once I returned to Gia's side, it was quiet again.

Mom stood next to Gia. "So, I see you two are really dating now."

"Yes, ma'am," Gia said.

"My only question for you, young lady, is…" Mom glanced at the rest of the women, then back at us. "What the hell took you so long?"

They all cackled at my mom's loud question and bear hug. She released Gia. "Girl, this boy waited for this moment since he first laid eyes on you. I felt bad for him when you moved away." Mom leaned in. "His little ass used to jack off to the thought of you."

"Ma!"

"What? You did! It's natural. Hush up." She hooked Gia's arm. "Come sit with us. You're already family. We about to play cards and this ain't your first rodeo."

Grandma looked up at me. "Who woulda thought the one time we meet one of this boy's lady friends that it'd turn out to be somebody we already knew. You and Janelle used to be connected at the hip as children. Now, you and Zakari are connected in the middle."

Gia's head fell back with a belly laugh that made me laugh off my grandma's craziness. The women in my family had no filter. It was nothing new to Gia.

"Girl, if he's anything like his grandfather, you won't be going nowhere." She winked. My aunties gave her dirty looks and covered their ears, telling her to stop being nasty. "Now if y'all daddy couldn't lay the pipe right, none of y'all would be here. Stop acting like y'all don't understand the power of some good dick."

"Grandma! Come on now. You are too old to be saying things like that."

"Oh, I got your old." She stuck up the middle finger and threw her half-empty bottle of water at me. I moved, so it flew past me. "Little nigga callin' me old. Go pick up my water bottle before I beat yo' ass."

My aunties sounded like some damn hyenas. Gia joined in with them. "Y'all are off the chain," she said.

"You are about to be chained down soon with that one. He ain't gonna let you go. You might as well change that last name now," Mom told her. "I'm gonna introduce you to everyone as my daughter-in-law from now on."

Gia shook her head, but wouldn't dare object. They'd do their hardest to prove her wrong if she did. We didn't need them to say anything else.

"Now, daughter-in-law, you can sit next to me. You remember how we used to do."

"Yes, I do, and I'm ready for it all. My momma and Mimi loved these get-togethers."

Mom pressed her lips together. "Yes, they did. Mimi was a little hustler. She took a lot of our money back then. God rest their souls."

Janelle and Trish joined the women at the table with some drinks. "Cameron is here with the drinks." They placed liquor bottles of all kinds on the table. Gia rolled her eyes and Janelle narrowed hers. "Be nice. He's really sorry," she said under her breath for privacy.

Cameron walked up with a case of water and ice. My dad followed behind him with two coolers to fill with ice and drinks. The tension was thick between Cameron and my lady. The both of us could have words with him, but we let it be.

Dad hugged my mom and kissed her. Grandma smiled. "Look at all the love in the air. Ain't it beautiful." She looked around at all of us, then stopped at Gia and me. "You two are the only ones with no rings. When y'all gonna get with the program?"

"Grandma, don't start."

"Oh, shut up. You wait too long and you'll watch

another man put a ring on her finger. Trust me. We can move on with a quickness when a man knows what he wants. You better get with it."

Gia's usually smart mouth had nothing to say. She raised her church finger and backed away. Everyone cracked up. "See. Y'all scaring my girl away. We'll be back when y'all chill."

I grabbed Gia's hand and led her to the trail. We walked along the lake and got a reasonable distance away from my family. She laughed at my momma, clowning my puberty days.

"That's disgusting, Zak."

"You don't say that when you're milking it."

"Eww! Why you gotta say it like that?"

"Why you act like you don't be all on my shit?"

"I mean, I might be. But still."

We found a bench and sat. Gia rested her head on my shoulder. "I cannot believe we are really doing this."

"You better believe that shit. This is it. Me and you."

"You and me. I think I finally believe."

# Zakari

EPILOGUE

ONE YEAR LATER

"Yo, I'ma kill Nelle." I joined Gia on the balcony.

We ate breakfast on my balcony this morning. Gia's view was a'ight. Since I had moved into our building, we argued about who had it the best. My view of the resort style pool area beat watching traffic and tall buildings. Less noise, quaint, and somewhat more privacy when things got a little nasty. With Gia, that was guaranteed.

"Thank you," she said when I set her third mimosa on the table. "What she do now?"

"Man, look!" I handed Gia my phone, showing her the media dump from Janelle and Cameron's wedding last week.

Gia burst out laughing. I saw nothing funny about the video that hundreds of people had the undeserved pleasure of watching. "I'm the one who should be tripping. I'm not. So, relax."

"Of course, you not. You look sexy as fuck, moving your ass in a circle. Nobody told you to do all that with that tight ass dress on."

Gia cackled in my face. "G, that shit ain't funny. It was bad enough when y'all did it for the guests. Nobody told her to share it with the world."

"I look good. You should be happy."

"Too damn good. I'ma have to fuck some niggas up in these comments. Talkin' bout 'who's the one in the front?' I don't play like that."

Gia rolled her eyes, sipping her mimosa. "Zakari, you know you can't stop people from looking at me, right? Why do you even care? You did what no other man could."

"What's that?"

"You got me all to yourself."

I stopped swiping through my sister's IG page. "Damn, right. You better know that shit." I leaned to her side for a kiss. "That's all mine right there."

"You stupid." Gia giggled and continued grazing over the bacon left over on the platter I set up for her. I cooked for her and everything. When I said the woman changed my ass, I meant in every sense on the word. Wasn't no way I woulda done this for anyone but Gia. She was my baby forever. One day, I'd make it official.

I reluctantly brought my attention to my phone again. Gia was plastered all over my sister's IG. Best friends did that and I had to let it go. My sister looked like an angel in her wedding dress, but my eyes stayed on my baby in the maid of honor dress. It differed slightly from the brides-maids but held on to her curves for dear life. Deep down, I felt like Janelle had done it on purpose.

Since being with Gia, we'd all learned how much of a jealous motherfucker I was. She brought that out of me because I'd had no reason to be jealous of anyone before. Men who saw her on my arm still checked my baby out. It had me on edge most of the night.

"This nigga."

"Who?"

"You little wannabe man." Gia rolled her eyes, knowing exactly who I meant.

I showed her all the pics of him gawking in the background. She laughed at the one of us dancing as he watched from his table. "That nigga." We laughed. "Enough with the phone, babe."

I put it face down on the table. "You right. That shit was funny how he thought he could slide in."

"It was until your ass jumped in the conversation. You always gotta make sure people know we're together. I was handling it."

"Hell, naw. I had to rub that shit in his face. Cameron's punk ass too."

"Zak, it was his wedding. Trevor is his friend. You are so childish." She mushed the side of my head.

"Maybe. At least I ain't him. Acting like he was tryna make a hoe a housewife."

"You were the hoe. You got turned into a house nigga." She scrunched her face before we cracked up. "That sounded horrible."

"Yeah, don't say that shit no more. I ain't nobody's house nigga."

"My point is you were the hoe, not me. You got more bodies than me. And more mileage."

"I'd say that's debatable, but I don't wanna know or hear about it. So, get off this shit."

"Aww, poor baby. You can't handle another man touching—"

"Gia, keep playing and I'ma cut you off."

"Please, I'd last longer than you."

"Shit, you right." I picked up the plates from the table.

"Let's go inside."

It was a little after eleven. We cleaned the kitchen and drove out to Galveston. My parents usually invited us out on Saturdays, but we'd declined this weekend. I wanted Gia to myself.

The past year had shed light on so much now that I had the one woman I thought I'd have to live without. Keeping her happy became the joy of each day I opened my eyes. Gianna fucking Jameson was my lady. I'd do everything in my power to keep it that way.

I knew her already. Learned her ways over the years and got acquainted with new ones she had developed when she'd went away. I prayed to God so much as a youngin' that I'd get her to like me one day. Of course, I believed prayer worked, but after years passed, I assumed God took that request as a joke. Now, this woman loved me back. I was ready for everything with her.

We walked on the shore, passing families and other couples. Gia showed off those thick thighs in short blue jean shorts and a tank top. In the simplest attire, she was hands-down the most gorgeous woman God ever created. I could simply watch her in her element every second of every day.

Everything I'd clowned Byron for, he returned each time I lit up when I talked about her. I got it. I finally understood what happiness with the woman meant for you was like.

"I'm still mad at you for not going with me on this trip." Gia bumped me a few steps away.

"G, I told you it's too close to our deadline at work. I can't leave until we land this client."

She stopped our stroll and walked further into the water. "It still sucks. We haven't gone on a vacation outside the country yet."

"Baby, we have all the time in the world. Next time, I promise." I wrapped my arms around her and pecked at her nose. "Stop acting like you don't want to be with your people. You skipped their vacations last year. Enjoy this time with them."

"I will, but I just wanted you with me. I can't take Janelle."

"Next time. Besides, I'm sure Blair doesn't want me tagging along. He wants these moments with you and the fam."

"I guess."

After I looked past the pain Blair caused Gia, he was a cool dude. My dad and I hung out with him a few times. I just saw him last week. He really loved Gia and God I was glad she had him in her life.

Without her mom and grandmother, she needed a connection with her blood. My family loved her, but having Blair and his family gave her more than I ever could. I didn't want to be her escape when she traveled with them.

$$\mathcal{G}ianna$$

"Um, why do I have a butler suite?" I asked Blair and Shana. "What do I need with a butler?"

Blair poked the inside of his cheek with his tongue. "So, we got...an upgrade for free. We thought you'd enjoy being taken care of."

"Okay, but y'all have kids. I can take a smaller room. It's bad enough you won't let me spend my money. That is too much."

Shana placed her hand on mine. "Gia, you mean everything to us. We want you to have a memorable vacation with us this year. Please, take the room. No fussing. We love you. Accept the upgrade."

I exhaled through my nose. "Fine. I guess I can use the butler experience since Zakari couldn't be here."

"He takes good care of you, huh?" she asked.

"Yes, he does. In every way possible."

"Alright, alright. Enough of that. How about you help us get the kids settled, then we'll check out your suite together?"

Negril was breathtaking. Our resort made me giddy. I needed this break and environment. When Shana suggested Jamaica, I only had one request. I'd wanted to avoid Montego Bay. Mimi and I had vacationed there and I wasn't ready to revisit the same spot.

Olivia and Jonah jumped on their beds until we left to explore my unnecessary two-bedroom suite. Blair smiled too damn much on our way there. He had something up his sleeve, but I couldn't put my finger on it. The man kept texting someone and for a second; I thought it was another woman. That went out the window when he showed Shana his phone and she giggled along with him. They only reminded me of Zakari. I'd call him as soon as I got a minute alone.

"This is it," Blair stated the obvious when we reached my door.

"Y'all better not be surprising me with nothing behind this door."

"We're not." Blair raised his hand while the other one covered his heart.

I opened the door and immediately had the wind knocked out of me. Shana and Blair both held me up when my legs tried to give out. "I know you lying?"

Everyone in the room held cameras in their hands, recording and taking pictures of me as I walked in. Janelle and Cameron on one side, her parents on the other. Shana and Blair joined in on the act once I'd regained my strength. A guy in a tux played the piano, but I could barely see through the tears forcing their exit.

I wiped my eyes as dry as I could get them. Once my eyes reached the man standing on the other side of the room, they blurred again. Two easels were on each side of Zakari. One was a photo of my mom and the other of Mimi. That ugly cry showed out after seeing them.

I froze, trying my hardest to keep my composure. Zak met me in the middle of the room and held me in his arms until I calmed myself. His kisses to my temples and forehead gave me a comfort I didn't think anyone could.

"Baby, you're supposed to cry like this after I say what I have to say."

We all laughed. I slowed my breathing to keep it together. Seeing all of my family here took me out for a minute. Zak made sure I was good before he continued with his plan.

"I'm gonna kill you for this."

"I know." He kissed my lips. "Gia, I swear I didn't think you'd cry like a baby, but I understand. I wanted the two people who meant the world to you to be here. There's no way I could do this without them."

"Thank you," I said, faintly.

"Man, I had this speech about how much I knew I wanted a forever with you when I first laid eyes on you. In elementary school. Fifth grade to be exact." Everybody chuckled at him, trying to get through it. "None of it matters. As you probably can tell, I want to wake up to that ugly cry every day."

I hit Zak's arm. "I can't stand you."

"I mean, even with that face, you are the most beautiful being in existence. Gia, I love your ass from your hair to your toes. You know that. I will fight and go to war for you and even with you if I have to. Sometimes you take it there." I rolled my eyes but nodded at the accuracy. "Baby, it's you and me. My future used to be far out of reach because I didn't have you. Once you finally came to your damn senses, I see everything clearly. You cussing me out before, during, and after our wedding. You cussing me out when you birth our babies. You especially cussing me out when I make you mad. I mean, y'all the get the gist. I wanna spend the rest of my life getting cussed out by you."

Even the piano player cracked up. "Ugh, you get on my damn nerves."

"See? Sorry kids, but your sister has a major potty mouth." Liv and Jonah laughed, even they knew I slipped up a few times. "Gianna Renae Jameson, I waited on this moment for so long that I couldn't do it anymore. I want you. I need you. After you went against everything you ever believed in and gave me the chance to prove my love to you, I promise to protect your heart. You will only know love from me. Nothing less. Will you make a man's lifelong dream come true and become my wife?"

I tilted my head to the side. "First, I am not the only one cussing people out. You are just as bad. Second, I thought you weren't saying your long ass speech. I was ready to say yes the moment I walked through the door."

The room chuckled and cheered. My husband-to-be lifted me and spun me around, kissing me the entire time.

Zak put me down and slid the ring on my finger. He did good. It was perfect.

"Congratulations! Daughter-in-law will finally be official." My future mother-in-law held me tightly. "I know Elaine and Eleanora are both smiling as hard as I am right now. I am so happy for you and my son."

"Thank you!" I hugged her again.

"Now, the race is on for one of y'all to give me some damn grandbabies. I don't have much time left. I'm getting so old." She had to nerve to move around like she was fragile.

"Ma! Don't do all that," Janelle said as she bumped her to the side to hug me next. "I knew you'd be my sister one day. Guess my brother broke the curse, huh?"

"Looks like it." I hated to admit but there was no need denying it now.

Blair and Shana cheesed so damn hard, it rubbed off. "We are so happy for you!"

"Thank you. Both of y'all lied though."

"A white lie. We couldn't ruin the surprise. Besides, Zak did it all on his own. We just had to get you to the room."

Zak came from behind and kissed my neck. "Don't give them a hard time. I had to do this right."

"You definitely did, babe." I turned to face him. "I love you, Zakari."

"Damn, I love hearing you say that shit. I love you more, Gianna." Our lips met again. "We gotta get these people outta here so we can practice grandbaby making."

"Practice only."

"Absolutely. We got time." Zakari brushed his bulge across my ass.

"Ay, um. Y'all gotsta go. We got some thangs to discuss," I told our family.

Zak's mom smiled too damn hard. "Y'all nasty, but do what you gotta do. I'm putting money on y'all giving me my first baby."

"Man, we'll see you later." Zak playfully pushed his parents out last.

We finally had the place to ourselves. "You really 'bout to be my wife?"

"I am. Unless you do something stupid."

"Still believe in your family curse?"

"Ugh, you and your damn sister." I laughed. "No, I don't. You've officially shown me the light."

"Shit, you and me both. Guess we both got a sip of the Kool-Aid."

"Red flavor."

"Damn, right."

THE END

Thank you for reading my first standalone! I hope you enjoyed Gia and Zak's story as much as I did writing it. These two got on my nerves with the back and forth lol. It was funny watching them go at it when they both wanted each other but denied it. Sometimes my fingers do the typing as I'm watching it all go down in my head.

Anyway, I'd truly appreciate if you leave a review. Readers take other reader's opinions to heart. Short and sweet or rants welcomed. I love learning how my characters made you feel. Thank you in advance.

# ACKNOWLEDGMENTS

Bridgette — I can't ever thank you enough. Your belief in me is one for the books. I love you so much and I'm forever grateful to have you in my corner.

R.A.M.s – Thank you for your true support. The emails I get from you telling me what you think of my stories and how they have touched you in some way will always be the greatest reward. That's the real reason why I won't stop. Love you all.

If you aren't a R.A.M. subscriber, get on it. I'd love to connect with you. You'll have direct access to tell me what you feel when you can't put it in a review. Sometimes that helps the both of us. Sign up @ bit.ly/RAMList

# ABOUT THE AUTHOR

Renée is from the best city on the planet—Houston. She resides there with her three kids. She writes fiction based on African American characters. Renée loves creating stories with relationship drama that can easily be found in many households. She wants readers to see themselves or recognize someone they know in her characters. If she can make you laugh, gasp, think, or even cry, then her mission will be accomplished.

Connect with Renée:
**www.authorramoses.com**
**www.facebook.com/authorramoses**
On Instagram @reneeamoses
On Twitter @authorramoses

Listen to Same Book, 3 Time Zones: A Book Review Podcast
We read one book a month and post our discussion.
**bit.ly/sb3tzYT**     **www.sb3tzreviews.com**
On Instagram @sb3tz_reviews

Signup for latest news, first looks, and exclusive content:
bit.ly/RAMList

**Turns in Love Series:**
*Two Lefts, One Right*
*Making a Hard Right*
*Straightaway*
*Wishing for Her*
*Truth Is…*

**Harris Sisters Series**
*The Cost of Loving You*
*I Thought I Knew You*
*Never Stopped Loving You*
*Not Good Enough For You*